HUNT
THE MAN
DOWN

Also by Lewis B. Patten

HUNT
THE MAN
DOWN

LEWIS B. PATTEN

DOUBLEDAY & COMPANY, INC.

GARDEN CITY, NEW YORK

1977

Library of Congress Cataloging in Publication Data

Patten, Lewis B
Hunt the man down.

(A Double D western)
I.   Title.
PZ4.P316Hu   [PS3566.A79]   813'.5'4

ISBN: 0-385-12890-8
Library of Congress Catalog Card Number 76-53414

HUNT
THE MAN
DOWN

CHAPTER ONE

The storm struck half an hour before dusk, with a sudden howling intensity that almost instantly filled the air with stinging particles of sleet, driven horizontally on a gale-strength wind, cutting visibility within minutes to fifty yards. The sleet pelted hard for ten minutes before it changed to small, stinging flakes of snow that thickened rapidly and quickly covered the ground except in the places where the wind had kept it scoured clean.

From a temperature of forty, it dropped to ten above in thirty minutes. The people of Chimney Rock hurried along the streets, coat collars turned up, heads ducked for protection from the wind. Horses in the corral at the livery barn crowded together and turned their rumps to the wind.

Mike Logan, who owned the livery stable, closed the big double doors at front and rear and dropped the bars into place. Wind howled in the building's eaves. The whole structure creaked whenever it was struck by a particularly strong gust. Mike went into the tackroom and shook down the ashes in the stove. He built a fresh fire, a worried expression on his face. This was the first bad storm of the year, and early. It was only October 28. He wondered if Martha Lansing and her two little kids, Frank and Julie, had enough firewood in the house. He hoped they had been inside when the storm struck and not out driving in the cows.

Martha was a widow who lived in a small log cabin about six miles north of town. Her husband had been dead nearly a year. She lived by milking half a dozen cows, by raising and canning garden vegetables in the summertime, and by canning venison from an occasional deer Mike killed and brought to her. For cash money, she did sewing for the ladies in town whenever they were willing to travel the six miles to her house.

She was a pretty woman, not yet twenty-five. She'd had suitors, but not many men were anxious to take on responsibility for two of someone else's kids. Mike was her steadiest visitor. He knew how she felt about waiting a decent interval after her husband's death. Most everyone considered a year a sufficient period of mourning, and so when the year was soon up, he intended to ask her to marry him. And he thought she would.

The tackroom warmed as the fire grew. Wind, blowing so hard across the metal chimney on the stable roof, made the fire draw extremely well and the stove began to roar. Its metal sides turned red.

Frowning, Mike Logan paced back and forth. Finally he made up his mind. If he didn't go out to Martha Lansing's place, he'd worry about her for the duration of the storm, which could be, from the looks of it, as much as a week.

With his mind made up, he closed the damper on the

stove and the vent at the bottom. He got his sheepskin from a nail, put on a pair of chaps, and pulled on his overshoes. He felt in the pocket of the sheepskin for his gloves.

He went out into the stable and selected the strongest of the horses in the stalls, a big, Roman-nosed gray. He saddled and bridled the animal, then led him up front to the tackroom door. He didn't know quite why he did it, but he thrust his 30-30 Winchester carbine down into the saddle boot after loading it.

He opened one of the front doors, led the reluctant horse out into the blasting, bitter wind, then closed the door behind him, securing it with a peg thrust down through the padlock hasp. He mounted, a little awkwardly because of the heavy coat and chaps.

Up through town he headed, taking the narrow road that led up the valley of Brush Creek, riding straight into the teeth of the howling wind.

In minutes his face was crusted with snow. His eyes were nearly blinded and he was forced to peer out through snow-encrusted slits. The horse fought him every inch of the way, but he kept drumming on the horse's sides with his heels and refusing to let the animal turn aside. Eventually, a couple of miles from town, the horse accepted the inevitable and stopped trying to turn back.

Landmarks had disappeared. Visibility was limited to the road itself, and only there because the wind kept some areas of it swept clean. But as darkness fell, Mike lost sight of everything and began to wonder if he would be able to find the turnoff to Martha Lansing's place. It was certain that no lamplight would be visible through this storm.

Nor would the turnoff itself be visible. He had gone what he judged was about six miles and was beginning to think he was a fool for having come when he heard what sounded like a faint scream, a sound quickly snatched away by the wind. The first thing that crossed his mind was that Martha had been out after the cows and had been caught by the storm. She was lost, and screaming into the void for help.

The scream had come from his right. Immediately he turned that way, leaving the road, kicking his horse into a trot. Within fifty feet, he came up against a barbed-wire fence. He turned left, following it, and as he did, he heard the scream again, able to place its location more exactly this time because it didn't take him by surprise.

The fence ended, and he knew he was in Martha Lansing's lane. Her cabin should become visible at any time. Faintly he glimpsed a light ahead and spurred his horse to a reckless gallop. Nearly to the cabin, he heard the scream again, and realized with a shock that it had come from inside the house.

He was off his horse in a leap, nearly falling because his legs were numb with cold. He stumbled toward the door, which was slightly ajar.

He flung it open, pausing just an instant, not expecting what he saw. Martha, her clothing half ripped from her body, was struggling frantically with a man. In a corner of the room her two small children cowered in terror, looking on.

Mike didn't recognize the man because the intruder's

back was toward him. He charged across the room, a wordless roar issuing from his mouth. With both hands, he seized the attacker's coat and yanked him back. There was the sound of tearing cloth as still more of Martha's clothing was ripped away, remaining in her attacker's hands.

Mike had never been so completely furious in his entire life. He flung the man across the room with a strength he hadn't known he possessed, slamming him against the wall beside the door with a crash that shook the building despite the fact that it was built of logs. His face contorted with rage, he lunged in pursuit.

And now he recognized the man. Reese Diamond, youngest son of the most powerful cowman in the country. Diamond seemed temporarily stunned, but he recovered quickly when he saw Mike Logan's face. He pushed himself to his feet, turned, and fled through the open door, with Mike in hot pursuit.

Diamond's horse was at the side of the house. Mike caught one of Diamond's legs as he hit the saddle, but the horse surged into motion and Mike was unable to hold on. He turned and sprinted for his own horse. He heard Martha scream at him to come back, but the sound only partially penetrated his consciousness. He hit the saddle, reined the horse around, and was, in an instant, in full gallop pursuing the fugitive.

The blizzard wind still howled. The air was thick with snow, driven horizontally on the wind. But Mike was only fifty feet behind the fugitive, mounted on a stronger horse, and gaining steadily.

Up the bed of Brush Creek the two horses thundered.

The lights and sounds of the cabin faded away behind. Mike didn't even think about what he was going to do when he caught up with Reese. He was too furious to think.

He lost his quarry half a dozen times in the first couple of miles, but each time, recklessness and the power of his horse made it possible for him to catch up. At last, nearly three miles from the Lansing cabin, the inevitable happened. Reese Diamond's horse's foot caught on the limb of a downed tree and he fell, throwing his rider clear. Mike, less than fifty feet behind, nearly overran both horse and man before he could yank his mount to a halt.

A tongue of flame lashed out at him from a black shape in the snow. The bullet struck his shoulder, burning like an iron. He left his horse instantly, but he grabbed the stock of his 30-30 as he did, and had it in his hands when he hit the ground. His horse went on for twenty or thirty yards before he stopped.

Mike, rolling on the ground in six inches of powder snow, saw the second tongue of flame. This bullet missed, but it gave Mike a target and he took instant advantage of it. He levered the carbine, and from a prone position fired at the flash.

He levered in a second shell, shifting position to his right as swiftly as he could in case Reese fired at his muzzle blast. But there was no sound.

In silence, Mike lay there nearly five minutes, suspecting Reese of setting a trap for him. Still nothing happened. Still there was no sound.

Finally, cautiously and aware of how terribly cold he was, Mike pushed himself stiffly to his feet. His hands were almost too numb to hold or pull the trigger of his gun, but he kept it pointed at the dark shape in the snow as he approached. He said, "Reese?" but no answer came.

Reaching the body, he stirred it with his boot. It was inert and yielding and he suddenly knew that Reese Diamond was dead.

He stooped and felt for Reese's pulse, detecting none. He started to take Reese's gun, but then he stopped. This was not an ordinary killing of a man caught in an attempted rape, a man who had subsequently tried to kill the one who had caught him in the act. It was more complicated than that, because Reese was who he was.

With uneasiness growing rapidly in him, Mike walked toward his horse. He caught the animal, then walked to where Reese's horse stood. Holding the reins of Reese's horse, he mounted his own and rode back toward Martha Lansing's cabin.

He had caught Reese Diamond trying to rape Martha in her own home. He had pursued him and Reese had fired first and wounded him. He was legally in the clear. But from past experience he knew that Jasper Diamond, Reese's father, didn't always do things legally. His youngest son was dead. He wasn't likely to accept a coroner's verdict of justifiable homicide. He would insist on wreaking a vengeance of his own. And that placed Mike in the most deadly danger he had ever experienced. Jasper Diamond had four remaining sons and a crew of seven men.

He reached Martha's cabin and dismounted from his horse. He was so cold he could hardly walk. His hands would scarcely function at all. He left both horses in the lee of the cabin, knowing they would remain there of their own accord. Then he rounded the house and knocked on the door.

Her voice was timid and scared. "Mike?"

"Uh-huh. It's me."

The door opened and he went inside. The two children looked at him as if they were afraid of him, too, although usually they ran to him. Martha had changed her torn clothing but the terror wasn't gone from her. She peered past Mike into the darkness as if expecting to see Reese reappear. In a scarcely audible voice she asked, "What happened? Where is he?"

"He's dead." Mike crossed to the stove, held his hands spread out toward it briefly, and then turned his back to it. His coat began to steam.

"Dead?" Martha's voice was shocked. She stood with her back to the door, staring at him in disbelief.

She was a head shorter than Mike, a slender woman, yet a woman with all the right curves in all the right places. An exciting woman, Mike thought. He loved her and he also loved her kids.

He turned around to face the stove again. His hands were beginning to hurt, and his face burned like fire. He took off his coat and hung it on the back of a chair. He said, "I chased him. I don't know why, because I knew who he was. I suppose if I thought about it at all, I figured he'd lie out of it unless he was actually caught out here."

Her eyes clung fearfully to his face and he could see that her thoughts were going beyond tonight to the consequences when Reese's father found out about his death.

Mike said, "I nearly lost him a couple of times—the storm's so bad—but finally his horse stumbled on a limb of a down tree that was buried in the snow. He fell and threw Reese and when I went toward him; he shot me." He half turned to show her the bloody shoulder of his shirt. Immediately, and with an expression of worried concern, she came to him, pushed him into a chair, then went to the kitchen range for hot water to wash the wound.

Mike felt drowsiness coming over him. He said, "I had my rifle and I shot back. Shot at the second flash of his gun. When I reached him he was dead."

"Shouldn't you have brought him in?"

"I thought about it. I decided if there was any chance at all of me being believed, I'd better leave him exactly like he was. I want you to save those torn clothes of yours, too. How'd he happen to be here anyway?"

"Just knocked on the door. Said he'd been caught in the storm and could he come in and get warm. He kept watching me and the first thing I knew he was pawing me. I fought him and he got more and more violent the more I resisted. That was when you broke in."

She brought a pan of warm water and some cloths for bandages ripped from some kind of cotton material. She also brought a small brown bottle of whiskey to disinfect the wound.

Mike gripped the sides of the chair while she worked on him. The two children, Frank, who was five, and Julie, who was three, came timidly from the corner to watch while she bandaged it. Frank asked fearfully, "Does it hurt?"

Mike grinned weakly. "Some." Right then he didn't care how much the bullet wound hurt. It was the only thing that could save his life. Without it, Jasper Diamond would claim that he had murdered Reese in cold blood, and as powerful as he was, he would probably make the accusation stick.

CHAPTER TWO

———◆———

Martha finally finished with the bandaging and helped Mike put the upper half of his underwear and his shirt back on. Every movement of his shoulder hurt. The bullet had gone through, missing arteries and bones, but tearing the powerful shoulder muscle.

The storm still howled without let-up outside. Mike asked, "Have you got enough wood in the house to last you two or three days?"

She nodded. He glanced at the woodbox beside the stove and saw that it was full and that there was a pile of wood beside it on the floor. "How about food?"

She smiled at his concern. "Enough."

"And the cows? Are they all in the shed, with plenty of hay?"

"Is that why you came out here? Because you were worried about us?"

"Sure. What's wrong with that?"

Her face sobered as she thought of Reese Diamond. "Nothing. I'm just awfully glad you did."

Mike got to his feet. His head whirled a little, but after

a moment or two the feeling passed. He said, "I've got to get back."

"You could stay. . . ." She stopped, her face flushing with embarrassment. Under ordinary circumstances maybe he could have stayed, but not with Reese Diamond lying out there dead in the snow. Jasper Diamond was going to make it look as ugly as he could anyway, and Mike's staying here overnight would only give him something to justify the accusations he was sure to make.

Mike bent and kissed each of the children on the head. They had lost their fear of him now that the shock of what had happened earlier had faded, at least partially, from their consciousnesses. Mike wanted to kiss Martha but he did not, knowing that the children would be questioned, and he didn't want something like a light, goodbye kiss blown all out of proportion later on.

Martha seemed to understand. She gave him a look that was warmer than any kiss and he went to the door. He put on his sheepskin while she held it for him, crammed his hat down so the wind wouldn't tear it off, and put on his gloves. He was warm now and the wind would be at his back all the way back to town.

When he opened the door, a blast of wind came in, carrying a swirl of snow halfway across the room. He smiled quickly at Martha, then closed it behind him. He heard the bar drop into place.

Both horses still stood patiently on the lee side of the house. Both saddles were covered with snow. Mike brushed off his own, picked up the reins of Diamond's horse, then mounted his own. Leading Reese Diamond's horse, he rode up the lane to the road.

Now, he knew, he could relax. He couldn't see any more than he had coming up, but he knew that the horse he was riding knew the way home and wouldn't stray from the road. He hunched down in the high collar of the sheepskin coat, and put one gloved hand in a pocket while he held the reins with the other one.

It was easier traveling with the wind. He got to wondering what Reese Diamond had been doing at Martha's house. Probably just heading toward town, or toward home, and got so cold he stopped there to get warm. Jasper Diamond would claim Martha had led him on, teased him and made him do what he had done. Mike felt himself getting angry just thinking of all the things Jasper Diamond was going to say. Before he was through, Martha would be the one on trial instead of Reese.

It was nine o'clock when Mike finally reached town. He was cold, but not as cold as he'd been whe he arrived at Martha's cabin earlier. He pulled up in front of the sheriff's office, tied his horse, and went inside.

Jack Bondy, the county sheriff, stood with his back to a red-hot stove. Wind swirled snow into the room and he said, "Shut the door!"

Mike did, and advanced across the room to the stove, pulling off his gloves. Bondy said, "This is a lulu. Where have you been?"

"Martha Lansing's place. I went up to make sure she had enough wood and food."

The sheriff grinned knowingly. "And did she?"

Mike didn't return the grin. He nodded. "Reese Diamond was there, trying to rip the clothes off her."

The sheriff's expression sobered. He studied Mike's face

with worried eyes, knowing there was more. "And you had a fight?"

"Sort of. He ran out the door, with me after him. He got to his horse and I took after him on mine. A few miles from the cabin, his horse took a fall."

"Is he hurt?"

"He's dead. He took a shot at me . . ." Mike turned to show the sheriff the bloody shoulder of his coat, "and I shot back. Actually, he shot at me twice. Hit me with the first. Gave me something to shoot at with the second."

"Oh, good God!" The sheriff's voice was shocked. "You're sure he's dead?"

"I felt for pulse. There wasn't any."

"Where is he? Did you bring him in?"

Mike shook his head. "Couldn't lift him with this shoulder wound. Besides, that storm is something awful. I'm not sure I could have loaded him even if I hadn't been hurt."

The sheriff was silent several moments, frowning, considering all the implications of what had happened to Reese Diamond. Finally he said, "There's going to be hell to pay. Reese was the old man's favorite."

Mike didn't say anything.

Bondy said, "And there weren't any witnesses?"

"How the hell could there be out there in that damned blizzard?"

"What's to keep old man Diamond from saying you fired first?"

"Because a dead man can't shoot back."

"I ought to put you in jail. You'll be safer there."

"Oh no! You put me in jail and everybody will assume I'm guilty."

The sheriff seemed to consider the pros and cons of that. Finally he shrugged. "He's going to have to be notified. Tonight."

"Don't look at me. If I went out there with news like that I'd be as dead as Reese."

Bondy uttered a disgusted obscenity. "Why the hell don't people pick decent weather to break the law?"

Mike Logan's shoulder was aching enough to make him edgy and irritable. "What the hell do you mean, break the law? Since when is defending yourself breaking the law?"

"You chased him, didn't you?"

"And what was I supposed to do, wave goodbye to him? You know how I feel about Martha Lansing."

Bondy shrugged. "All right, all right." He closed the damper on the stove, crossed the room and got his coat, then sat down, took off his spurs and pulled on his overshoes. Mike said, "You'd better get Sid to go with you. Man hadn't ought to be out there all by himself."

"I'll be all right."

Mike said, "You can't even see the side of the road. If I hadn't heard Martha scream, I'd probably have ridden right on past."

Bondy nodded. "All right. Go tell him to come down here right away. Tell him to put on all the warm clothes he's got, including chaps and overshoes."

Mike nodded, crossed the room, and went out into the storm, closing the door quickly behind him.

Bondy finished putting on his overshoes, an angry scowl on his face. He didn't want to go out in this storm.

Not only was it uncomfortable; it was dangerous. A man could get lost, and if he did, he'd freeze to death. Briefly he considered waiting until morning, and discarded the idea. Jasper Diamond would only be further infuriated if Reese was allowed to lie out there all night and freeze as stiff as a board.

He supposed he'd have to rely on the horses to find the road and stay on it. He suddenly remembered that Jasper Diamond had a couple of buckboard horses down at the livery stable that he'd brought in to be shod. They'd know the way home, storm or no storm, and it would be a hell of a lot more comfortable for him and Sid on the buckboard seat than it would in a saddle. They could protect themselves with blankets and huddle together for warmth.

Nervously he paced back and forth, waiting for Mike to return with Sid DeVoe. It was a dozen miles to the Diamond place, and it would all be straight into the wind. It sounded to him like Mike had been justified in what he'd done, and he knew Mike well enough to know that what he'd said was the truth. But he also knew Jasper Diamond and he knew how much Diamond had cared for his youngest son, the reckless one, the one who was always in trouble with women, or involved in a fight because he didn't know how much liquor he could hold.

Jasper Diamond had seemed to take a kind of strange pride in Reese's high-spirited antics. Maybe in Reese he saw a lot of himself when he'd been that age. He must have been like Reese when he was young, the sheriff thought. He'd worn out four wives. His fifth wife, the one to whom he was married now, hadn't been able to present him with any children. Whether that was Jasper's fault or hers nobody knew, of course, but the chances were that it was hers. Or maybe Jasper was just too old to father any more children. Nobody knew his exact age, but Bondy guessed he must be seventy at least.

The door opened, letting in a blinding cloud of snow and a gust of bitter wind. Sid DeVoe and Mike Logan came in and slammed the door.

Sid was bundled up in chaps, overshoes, sheepskin, and woolen stocking cap. He had a couple of blankets under one arm and carried a rifle in his other hand. Bondy said, "Mike, go down to your stable and get those two buckboard horses that Diamond left last week to be shod. Hitch them to a buckboard and bring it here."

Mike nodded and went out. Sid stared at Jack. "Mike says he killed Reese Diamond. Is that true?"

"It's true."

"Over what? He didn't say."

"Mike went out to Martha Lansing's place to see if she was all right. He caught Reese trying to tear the clothes off of her. Reese ran and Mike took after him."

"There's a hole in the shoulder of Mike's coat and a lot of blood."

"Reese shot Mike just before Mike shot him."

"Old man Diamond isn't going to believe that."

"I know it."

Sid whistled. "I sure wouldn't want to be in Mike Logan's boots."

Bondy didn't reply. He got a rifle from the rack, loaded it, then gathered up the blankets from the office cot. By the time he had finished, he heard the buckboard outside the door. He said, "All right, let's go. These horses know their way home, so we shouldn't run much risk of getting lost."

Bondy blew out both office lamps and the two men went out. Bondy climbed to the seat of the buckboard and took the reins from Mike. He said, "Go home. Where is Reese's body, by the way, in case old man Diamond wants to go get it yet tonight?"

"Upstream from Martha's place about three miles. It's on the west side of the creek and no more than a dozen feet from it."

Sid was arranging the blankets to give both men some protection from the wind. Bondy nodded, took the whip out of the socket, and laid it on the backs of the horses, one after the other.

The jail and Mike, standing in the driving snow, faded away behind. For a little while the horses fought against traveling straight into the wind, but by the time Bondy got them out onto the road, they realized they were going home and stopped trying to turn back.

Huddled on the seat, Bondy and Sid DeVoe peered out through slits they had arranged in the blankets. Bondy cursed sourly beneath his breath.

It wasn't just the storm, although that was bad enough. It was what lay ahead that worried him. Jasper Diamond was a man with an unbridled temper. He was used to having his way. He'd settled in this country thirty years ago when there still were small foraging parties of quarrelsome Indians around from time to time. He'd killed a couple of them that he caught in his smokehouse and there'd been a big stink about it, but he'd never gone to trial. He'd hanged a horse thief once before Bondy had become sheriff and he'd shot a couple of rustlers, crippling one of them for life.

He still thought the same way he had when he first settled here. He preferred to make and enforce his own laws rather than rely on the sheriff and the courts.

And Bondy had a sneaking feeling that he was going to do just that in the case of his son Reese's death. He would catch Mike Logan, try, convict, and execute him, and to hell with whatever the later consequences of it might be.

But times had changed. He could no longer make and enforce his own law. He might go to prison for killing Mike, but that wasn't going to help Mike.

What he ought to do, Bondy thought, was arrest Jasper Diamond and throw *him* in jail until the worst of his fury had passed. He also knew that he could not. In the first place, Jasper Diamond had done nothing wrong. Lester Miller, the town lawyer, would have him out before it got light tomorrow.

In the second place, even if he could hold Diamond in jail, it wouldn't change anything. Diamond still had four sons. They did what he told them to. If he said find Mike Logan and kill him, that was exactly what they would do.

CHAPTER THREE

The drive out to the Diamond Ranch seemed to take forever. There was no let-up in the storm. If anything, the wind seemed to have increased its intensity. Snow drifted in places across the road until it was all the two horses could do to fight through it and drag the buckboard through. Bondy wondered how they did it, staying on the road, never even putting a wheel of the buckboard off the edge. He supposed they had an instinct for it.

He marked their progress by the bridges they crossed and by the dry washes they descended into and climbed out of again. At last the team turned down into the lane that led to the Diamond Ranch, and after another few minutes Bondy saw the faint flickering of lights.

He drove past the house and straight into the barn but he didn't unhitch the horses. He climbed stiffly down and Sid followed suit. They had either been seen or heard passing the house. The back door opened and old man Diamond and three of his sons came hurrying out, shrugging into coats and cramming on hats as they did. They came into the barn. Hank Diamond had a lighted lantern and by its light Jasper and his sons could see who the visitors were.

The old man asked harshly, "What the hell brings you out here in this godawful storm?" It was a normal enough question under the circumstances, but Bondy thought he detected a note of concern in the old man's voice. Jasper knew Reese was off someplace and apparently the only reason he could think of to explain the sheriff's presence was that something had happened to Reese.

Bondy didn't see any sense beating around the bush. It was going to be a long enough night anyway. He said, "Reese has been shot. He's dead."

"Shot?" Outrage was the first emotion apparent in the old man's voice. "Shot by who? And why? You must've made a mistake. Reese couldn't be dead. Why, hell, I saw him around noon. It must be somebody else."

"Mike said it was Reese."

"Mike Logan? What has he got to do with it?"

"Mike's the one that shot him. In self-defense. Mike has got a bullet hole in his shoulder that Reese put there."

There was a silence that lasted nearly a minute. When the old man's voice came again there was a strange quality to it. Its tone showed both his shock and his grief, but it also revealed something else. An ominous note that boded no good for the killer of his son. Diamond said, "I think you'd better let me have it from the beginning." He glanced around at his sons. "Saddle up. We've got work to do."

They moved away. Bondy said, "Mike went out to Martha Lansing's house when the storm got to looking bad to make sure she had enough wood in the house and that she hadn't got caught outside driving in the cows. He heard her screaming and when he went in the house, Reese was fighting with her, trying to rip the clothes off her."

"That's a goddamn lie! Reese don't have to rip the clothes off no woman. They take 'em off for him."

Bondy felt a touch of irritation at the old man's arrogance. He asked, "You want to hear this or not?"

"Don't get smart with me!"

"Then keep your mouth shut until I'm through." Bondy was cold all the way to the marrow of his bones. He knew they were going to have to go back out into the storm and search until they found Reese's body, which might take a long time because by now the snow would have drifted over him. Bondy said, "Logan had a fight with him, and Reese ran out into the snow. Got on his horse and took off, with Logan after him. Logan says he chased him about three miles up the creek before Reese's horse caught his foot on something and fell. Reese was thrown. He took a shot at Logan and got him in the shoulder."

"Too bad he didn't get him in the head."

Bondy stared irritably at him. He waited a moment and then went on. "Reese fired at him again after Logan had left his horse. Missed. Logan fired at the flash and I guess that's the one that killed Reese. Logan brought his horse and came back to town."

"Why the hell didn't he bring Reese?"

"He was shot in the shoulder, that's why. And Reese must weigh a couple of hundred pounds."

Diamond's sons were now bringing horses, bridled but not yet saddled. The other son, Lentz, came from the house to see what was going on. Diamond told him to unhitch the buckboard team. He did, and led the horses away.

It took maybe twenty minutes to saddle seven horses. When the job was done, Diamond said to his sons, "Go on in the house and get whatever coats and caps and gloves you think you're going to need. We might be out a while."

They dispersed. Diamond asked, "Where's Logan now?"

"I sent him home."

"He's not in jail?"

"Why should he be in jail? If his story's true, all he did was defend himself."

"*If* his story's true."

Diamond's four sons had come from the house and now stood waiting, wearing heavy sheepskin coats, chaps, overshoes, and gloves. Two had their regular hats on. The others wore woolen stocking caps. Diamond said, "We'll need a horse with a packsaddle to bring Reese's body into town."

Lentz went to get another horse. Bondy said, "What about your wife? Hadn't you ought to tell her what's going on?"

"Why? Reese ain't her kid."

Bondy shrugged. Here in the barn, out of the bitter wind, he had warmed somewhat. He mounted the horse that had been provided for him and Sid DeVoe mounted his. They waited and let old man Diamond lead off. His sons fell in behind according to age. Bondy and Sid brought up the rear, staying close enough so that they couldn't lose sight of the men ahead of them. Diamond seemed to have no trouble staying in the road.

Bondy wrapped the blankets around his shoulder and brought them up over his head. It wasn't so cold riding with the wind, and the blankets helped. He felt drowsy but he wasn't really uncomfortable except for his hands, which were so cold they were numb. He alternated, putting one into the pocket of his sheepskin awhile and holding the reins with the other, then switching hands.

With the wind at their backs, the horses moved with more alacrity. They seemed to think they were headed for town. It wasn't very far from the Diamond place to Martha Lansing's place and Diamond seemed to have no trouble finding the lane. He turned in, with the whole cavalcade following. He didn't stop at the house, or even slow; despite the fact that the door opened and Martha peered fearfully out, an old muzzle-loader in her hands.

Bondy yelled at Sid, "Go with them. I want to talk to Mrs. Lansing."

He got no response from Sid, or if he did, the wind snatched the words away. He dismounted, already so cold he could hardly walk, and led his horse to the lee side of the cabin. Martha still stood in the doorway. Bondy took off his hat and batted it against his coat and chaps to at least partially get the snow off him. He asked, "Can I come in?"

"Of course." He went in and she closed the door. Bondy stood beside the door and shed his coat, chaps, gloves, and hat. He sat down in a chair and took off his overshoes. Then he crossed to the stove and spread his numbing hands to the welcome heat. He said, "That was Jasper Diamond and his four remaining sons."

Somehow or other he couldn't see this woman leading anybody on, let alone anybody as crude and direct as Reese Diamond. Her face, while not exactly beautiful, was very attractive. She had high cheekbones, somewhat hollow cheeks, a high, smooth forehead, and a straight, almost perfect nose. Her mouth was full, always seeming on the point of smiling, and her eyes were honest and direct.

Her body, while slight, was so formed so that he could see why it would excite Reese or any other man. She'd have twice the suitors she had, he knew, if it wasn't for the kids. He asked, "The kids in bed?"

She nodded. "They had a hard time going to sleep. After what happened, they were both pretty scared."

He lowered his voice. "Then I'll try not to waken them."

She looked at him questioningly.

Bondy said, holding his voice down, "Jasper Diamond is upset over the death of his son."

She nodded. "I can understand that."

"Logan should never have chased him."

Her face flushed slightly. "What should he have done, sheriff? Who would have believed, tomorrow, that Reese Diamond did what he did? And he'd have come back. If he'd try it once, he'd try it again."

"What exactly did happen, Mrs. Lansing?"

Her face flushed a darker shade. Bondy said, "I'm sorry, but I have to ask. The lawyers are going to ask when Logan comes to trial."

"Comes to trial? For defending himself?"

"He didn't have to chase Reese."

Her face stayed dark, but now her eyes flashed with anger. But she said calmly enough, "He knocked on the door. I opened it and let him in. After all, this is a pretty bad storm. What kind of woman would I be if I refused to let him in?"

"Yes, ma'am. Go on."

"He came in. He'd been drinking and he had a bottle in the pocket of his coat. He asked me to have a drink with him but I refused. I offered him something to eat but he said he wasn't hungry. He said he'd been watching me for a long time and," she paused uncomfortably, then said, "he thought by now I needed a man pretty bad."

"Then what?"

"I didn't like the way the talk was going and the way he looked at me frightened me. I told him to leave. He said he'd leave when he'd got what he came here for. I got up, pretending to go to the stove, and got that old gun my husband had. It wasn't loaded but I thought maybe it would scare him off. It had the opposite effect. He rushed me, tore the gun out of my hands, and began tearing at my clothes. The children were terrified. I fought him, but he was too strong for me."

"Logan says he heard some screams."

"I don't remember. I suppose I did scream. The door had blown partway open, because Mr. Diamond hadn't closed it tight. Anyway, it was about then that Mike—Mr. Logan came bursting in. He yanked Mr. Diamond away from me and threw him across the room. Before he could get to him, Mr. Diamond ran out the door and Mike ran after him. That was all I heard or saw until Mike came back with a bullet wound in his shoulder and told me Reese Diamond was dead."

Bondy nodded. He hemmed and hawed a little with embarrassment, then finally asked, "Ma'am, could I have the clothes that Reese Diamond tore? I don't know how sticky this thing is going to get, but I do know that Mike is going to have to prove everything he's said."

Martha Lansing's face had, by now, gone pale. She nodded wordlessly, got up, and went into the bedroom where she and the children apparently slept. She opened the door very quietly, tiptoed in, and returned a moment later, some torn clothing in her arms. She closed the door with equal care.

She handed the clothes to the sheriff, who rolled them up tightly. She seemed to understand that he wanted something to wrap them in, so she got him what was left of the sheet with which she'd bandaged Mike and a piece of twine to tie the bundle with.

Now, with equal embarrassment, the sheriff asked, "Did he put any marks on you, ma'am, and did you put any on him? Things like scratches, or bruises."

She sat there mute and immobile for what seemed a long, long time. Then, her eyes averted, she bared one shoulder by pulling her gown down over it. There, plain and unmistakable, were the bruised, blue marks of a man's fingers. She pulled the dress back up, and bared the other shoulder similarly. The same marks were visible there. Bondy asked, "Anything else?"

Angrily she asked, "What else should there be? He was tearing at my clothes. He still hadn't gotten them off."

"Sorry. How about him? Are there any scratches on him?"

"There most certainly are," she said spiritedly. "On his face and probably on his neck. I knew I didn't have much chance but I certainly didn't intend to make it easy for him!"

"No, ma'am." Bondy grew silent, listening. He knew it was still too soon for the others to be returning, unless they'd found Reese's body immediately.

Obviously relieved that the questioning was over, she now asked worriedly, "What's going to happen to Mike?"

Bondy shrugged. "He shouldn't have chased Reese, but Reese *did* shoot first. Mike only fired back in self-defense. He ought to come out all right as far as the law's concerned."

"What do you mean by that?"

He hesitated, then decided she might as well know the worst. He said, "Jasper Diamond has been making his own law hereabouts for a good many years, and Reese was his favorite." He didn't say any more. He didn't have to. He could tell that Martha Lansing had heard all the stories about Jasper Diamond and the times he had taken the law into his own hands. Her eyes were filled with fear.

CHAPTER FOUR

It was almost midnight before Bondy and Martha Lansing heard the sounds of men and horses outside the door. Nobody dismounted. Diamond just roared, "Bondy! Come on to hell out of there and let's get on to town."

Bondy began putting on his outer clothes, his chaps, overshoes, coat, and hat. He pulled on his gloves, then gathered up the now-wet blankets he had taken from the cot inside the jail and the package of clothing Martha had given him. He wanted to reassure Martha Lansing because she was a nice woman doing the best she could to survive and raise her kids without the help of any man. But there was nothing honestly reassuring he could say. He said, "Try not to worry," and went on out. He got his horse from the lee of the cabin, mounted, and followed the cavalcade toward town. He could see the lumpy shape of Reese Diamond tied across the packsaddle and he could feel the fury in all these men, with the exception of Sid, his deputy.

His own opinion was that Reese had gotten exactly what he deserved. Martha Lansing probably didn't weigh more than a hundred and fifteen pounds. Reese weighed nearly two hundred. Besides that, a decent widow with small children ought to be safe, and if she wasn't, then something sure as hell ought to be done to make sure she was. Mike Logan had done it, and Bondy felt a reluctant admiration for him, despite his fear that Mike would live to regret what he'd done. Or die regretting it.

The trip to town seemed endless. The storm had not abated. The wind still blew the snow horizontally to the ground. In the lee of every obstruction it had drifted from two to ten feet deep. Dry washes that ran east and west were filled with it. The drop-offs at the side of the road were sometimes level with the road. Once or twice, Jasper Diamond, leading, got off the road and they all floundered in snow deeper than their horses' bellies, but eventually each time they regained the road.

Bondy was glad to see the few scattered lights in town. Most of the inhabitants had gone to bed, of course, but a few lamps still burned.

Bondy ranged up beside Sid and slapped him on the back. "Let's go to the jail. They'll take care of Reese."

Sid followed him as he left the cavalcade and headed for the jail. Diamond went on, heading for Halliburton's Furniture Store and Undertaking Establishment.

Bondy and Sid went into the jail. The sheriff glanced at the clock, amazed to see that it was only one o'clock. Bondy lighted two lamps, took off his heavy sheepskin, already dripping with melted snow, and hung it on the coat rack, from which it dripped steadily to the floor as the heat melted more and more of the snow encrusted on it. He batted his hat against his leg to shake loose the snow, then hung the hat on top of the coat. The soggy gloves he spread out on a bare spot on his desk, palms up since the palms were wetter than the backs.

Before taking off his overshoes, he built up a new fire in the stove, opened damper and vent, and stood there a moment warming himself, listening to the roar of the stove. It occurred to him that he'd had no supper, and he was hungry but he didn't know where the hell he'd get anything to eat at this hour. Unless the saloon . . .

He glanced at Sid, just now shrugging out of his coat. "Is the Pink Lady still open?"

Sid DeVoe nodded. Sid was a scrawny, wizened man of maybe forty-five, with sparse yellow hair and a scraggly, droopy mustache. His eyes were blue and he had a perpetually weary and disillusioned look to him. He was only a part-time deputy. The rest of the time he was a saddlemaker and had a shop half a block down the street from the jail. Made damn good saddles, too, thought Bondy. Good, hardwood trees put together with pegs and covered with shrunk rawhide. You could rope a thousand-pound steer from one of Sid's saddles, and while the cinch might break, the tree never would.

Bondy said, "Go on over there and get a bottle. Load up something from the free lunch counter. Tell Condon neither of us got any supper tonight and that we're hungry as hell."

Sid shrugged back into his coat without comment. He crammed on his hat, buttoned his coat, then went out into the wind, still blowing horizontally straight down the street. Bondy watched him lean into it as he crossed the street and entered the Pink Lady Saloon.

He sat down and pulled off his overshoes. He knew

Jasper Diamond and his sons would be here as soon as they'd left Reese's body at the undertaker and made arrangements for the burial, which would, naturally, have to wait on the cessation of the storm. The ground wasn't frozen yet, of course, but you couldn't bury a man in a blizzard like this one. Not if you wanted people to turn out for it. And it looked to Bondy as if this storm might last for several days.

He put his back to the stove, which was now putting out a lot of heat, slowly taking the chill off the room. There was a chill in the sheriff too, also slow to dissipate and not entirely caused by the cold. He kept wondering what Jasper Diamond was going to do about Mike Logan. He knew damned well Diamond wasn't going to just sit back and let the law take its course. He himself had already told Diamond it looked like a case of self-defense.

Sid returned with a bottle and a paper bag filled with things from the free lunch counter. He ripped open the bag and spread its contents out on the sheriff's desk. There was sliced cheese, sliced ham, sliced roast beef, and plenty of bread cut in thick slices. Bondy made himself a sandwich so thick he could hardly take a bite of it, poured himself a drink into one of two glasses he took from the drawer of his desk, and began to eat. Sid followed suit.

The wind continued to howl. Snow, brought in by both men, melted on the floor, leaving puddles there.

Sid said, "Old man Diamond will be back."

"I know it. That's what I'm waiting for."

"What are you going to tell him?"

"To leave Mike Logan alone."

Sid stared at him ruefully. "Have him tell this damned blizzard to stop, while you're at it."

Bondy's shoulders sagged. He'd be about as successful doing one thing as the other. But what could he do? He and Sid weren't going to be able to stop Jasper Diamond and his four sons and his crew. And he wasn't going to be able to get any help. By the time help got here, even if he *could* get it, it would be too late. The best thing, he thought, would be to tell Mike Logan to get out of town. At least until Jasper Diamond buried his son and cooled off a bit.

Once more his mouth twisted sourly. Mike was as stubborn as Diamond was. Mike wouldn't leave, even if this storm didn't make it impossible. Mike didn't figure he'd done anything wrong in defending himself and he'd refuse to leave. But he had done something wrong, no matter how much he protested that he had not. He had pursued Reese Diamond when he could have let him go. It was understandable, of course, considering the way he felt about Martha Lansing, but if he hadn't done it, Reese Diamond would still be alive. And, the sheriff admitted reluctantly, Martha Lansing would still be in danger from him. An attempt to arrest Reese for attempted rape, bring him to trial, and get him convicted would be just about as useless as trying to warm up the whole town with his one little stove.

A bunch of horses pounded up to the rail in front of the jail. Jasper Diamond, crusted with snow that had built up on his coat between the undertaker's and here, slammed open the door and came in, followed by his four remaining sons. Bondy tried to look at him sympathetically but found it difficult. Diamond rasped, "He hunted my boy down like a goddamn wolf!"

Bondy didn't see any use in arguing. Diamond was furious and nothing would please him better than an argument. Sid backed into a corner of the room, sandwich in one hand, half-filled glass of whiskey in the other.

Diamond said icily, "I want him arrested and brought to trial!"

Bondy shook his head. "I can't arrest a man for defending himself."

"Defending himself? The sonofabitch . . . !"

Bondy asked, "Where was Reese shot?"

"Dead center in the chest."

"Then he was dead the minute he was hit. He couldn't have fired at Mike afterward."

"Maybe not, but . . ."

"The way Mike tells it, Reese fired at him twice. The first one hit Mike in the shoulder. The second gave him something to shoot at. I don't see how the hell you can get anything but self-defense out of that."

"Then I'll handle it myself." That idea seemed to be growing in Diamond's mind. "You find Mike Logan. You tell him that come daylight, me and my boys are going to hunt him down like a wolf. Just the way he hunted Reese."

"You do that and I'll have to come after you." It was weak and Bondy knew it was. Diamond was above the law in the county and had always been.

Diamond laughed contemptuously. He said, "You tell him. Because come daylight I'm going to his house and if he's there he's dead."

He glared at Bondy for a moment more. Bondy didn't say anything because there wasn't anything to say. Diamond would do exactly what he said he would, and Bondy, even with the help of Sid DeVoe, couldn't stop him. Diamond whirled on his heel and tramped out of the office. His four sons followed, reminding Bondy in that instant of young wolves, following the old, dominant male. They untied their horses, mounted, and galloped the block and a half to the three-story Plains Hotel.

Bondy had a moment's wry amusement as he wondered what they were going to do with their horses for the night. He needn't have bothered. One of Diamond's sons took the reins of the other four horses, as well as those of the packhorse that had brought Reese's body in. He headed downstreet toward the livery barn.

Bondy went outside and untied the two horses he and Sid had ridden here. As Hank Diamond passed, he hailed him and tied the reins of the two horses to the tails of two of the horses Hank was leading toward the livery.

Chilled, he hurried back inside. Fury at Mike Logan didn't keep Jasper Diamond from being practical. The Logan Livery Stable was the only one in town and he knew his horses needed to be in out of the storm.

Wearily, Bondy finished his sandwich, poured himself another drink of whiskey, downed it, and shrugged into his still-damp coat. "I'd better go see Mike," he said. "You can go on home if you want. There's nothing more to do."

Sid nodded. "Want me to blow out the lamps?"

"Blow out one. And close the damper on the stove. I think I'll spend the night right here."

He finished buttoning his coat, put on his hat, then sat

down and pulled on his overshoes. He got his damp
gloves from the desk and put them on too.

He wasn't proud of what he had to do. But if he didn't
do it, Diamond would keep his word. He'd go to Mike's
house tomorrow and shoot him down the same way he
would a wolf.

Maybe he could keep Mike alive awhile by throwing
him in jail. But that could backfire too. Diamond had the
money to hire the best lawyers in the state. He was owed
more than one favor by the governor and by other
officials of the state. He knew most of the judges and had
entertained them at his house, or had been entertained at
theirs.

He could get Mike Logan convicted of murder if he
was willing to try hard enough. He'd ruin Martha Lansing by making it look like she was the local whore.

Muttering savage, helpless curses, Sheriff Bondy
tramped along the snow-swept street in the direction of
Mike Logan's house.

CHAPTER FIVE

———————◆◆◆———————

Mike Logan lived in a two-room frame house on the street behind the livery stable and about half a block north of it. It was a typical bachelor's house, its picket fence missing nearly as many pickets as it possessed and needing paint badly. The grass was long and uncut, liberally sprinkled with weeds, some of which were as much as two feet high, when not covered with snow.

The porch sagged and the boards creaked as Bondy crossed it to the door. There was a lamp burning inside. A loose roof shingle flapped incessantly in the wind, which continued to howl. The snow began to drift deeply in the lee of everything that broke its force.

Mike Logan opened the door and Bondy went in immediately, closing the door behind him. A swirl of snow accompanied him in, melting as quickly as it struck the floor.

Mike didn't ask what had brought the sheriff out. He knew. He asked, "Coffee?" Bondy glanced at the stove and at the pot sitting on top of it. He guessed, rightly, that the coffee would taste like lye, but he was cold and he nodded. Mike got a tin cup and poured it full. Bondy sipped it, burning his lips on the tin cup and saying irrita-bly, "For Christ's sake, is tin cups all you've got?"

"The others are dirty."

"You sure need a wife."

Mike grinned at him disarmingly. He was a big man, six feet one inch tall. His shoulders were broad and strong, his chest deep. His hips were narrow, his legs a little short for the rest of him. A man, Bondy thought, who had done hard physical work all his life and had the body to show for it.

Mike's face was as lean and spare as the rest of him, with hollow cheeks below high cheekbones and a rather thin-lipped mouth that could and often did break into a warm and disarming smile. Bondy liked Mike. Everybody did. There wasn't anything about him to dislike.

Bondy said, "Jasper Diamond and his sons stopped at the jail after leaving off Reese's body at the undertaking parlor."

Mike asked the obvious question. "What did they want?"

"Wanted you arrested and charged with murder."

A wary expression came to Mike Logan's eyes. "Is that why you're here?"

Bondy shook his shaggy head. "There's not enough evi-dence to convict you, and besides, if I put you in jail ev-erybody would start thinking you were guilty."

"So what are you going to do?"

"I'm not going to do anything. I came here to tell you what you've got to do."

"And what is that?"

"Run. Diamond served notice on me that he was coming here at daylight and that if you were still here, you were dead. He says you hunted Reese down like a wolf and that's exactly what he's going to do to you."

"You're the sheriff. Stop him."

Bondy laughed bitterly. "Stop Jasper Diamond and those four sons of his?"

"So what are you doing here?"

"Just telling you. If you stay here tonight, they'll kill you in the morning."

"And you won't stop them."

"How can I stop them? There's five of them. I'll arrest whoever does it afterward, but you know how much good that's going to do. Besides, you'll already be dead."

"Then what's your advice?"

"Get the two best horses you've got. Turn the others out. By morning, there won't be any trail. I'll pry a shoe off each of the Diamond horses and throw it away. That'll slow them down a little bit."

"You sure as hell don't give a man much choice."

"What choice is there? Jasper Diamond says he's going to hunt you down like a wolf and that's exactly what he'll do. Not only that, he'll get away with it. He'll claim Martha Lansing is . . . well, that she led Reese on. He'll claim that you shot him in cold blood and that you were hit by a bullet he fired as he fell. He's got a lot of influence and a lot of money. He'll make it stick, because he'll buy judges and juries and witnesses."

"What about my livery barn?"

"I'll get somebody to run it for you. Eventually, Diamond will cool down. You can come back when he does.

I'll write to you care of general delivery in Custer City when I think it's safe."

There was a bitterly angry expression on Mike Logan's face. He'd done only what any decent man would do. Catching Reese Diamond attempting to rape Martha in front of both her small children, he'd chased him out of the house, pursued him, and defended himself when Reese wounded him. Now he had to run because Reese's father was not only wealthy but a power in the community and in the state.

But Logan was not a fool. He knew staying was the equivalent of accepting death. He shrugged. "All right. I'll go. Give me a few minutes to get some things together."

He went into the kitchen, found a gunnysack, and filled it with what provisions he had in the house. Staples like beans, sugar, salt, salt pork, some old jerky with dust on it, flour, a can half full of lard, and a few other things. In a second gunnysack he put frying pan, skillet, coffeepot, enameled plate, and a clean tin cup as well as a butcher knife, fork, and spoon. Then got himself some blankets, which he wrapped in an oilcloth slicker and tied with a piece of rope.

He already had his Winchester leaning against the wall beside the door. He got several boxes of cartridges for it, and got his revolver, which he hadn't worn for years, and strapped it around his waist.

He shrugged into his heavy sheepskin coat, which was still damp on the outside even though the inside was dry. He pulled on his chaps and overshoes, got saddlebags and put into them what money he had, and some clean under-

wear, socks, and shirts. He put the extra rifle shells into
one of the gunnysacks. He looked at Bondy. "I guess
that's all."

"I'll go down to the stable with you."

Mike nodded. He blew out the lamps, followed Bondy
out the door into the savage wind, and closed and locked
the door behind him. The two walked abreast along the
street, then cut through the vacant lot to the rear stable
door. The corral had half a dozen horses in it. Mike
opened the gate to let them out. They'd find shelter in the
creek bottom, and would be able to paw the snow off
enough grass to keep them alive.

Neither man lighted a lamp inside the stable. The Dia-
monds were at the hotel, but if they saw light in the stable they might guess what was going on. Mike selected
the two strongest horses. He saddled and bridled one, put
halter and packsaddle on the second. He tied on his gunnysacks and blanket roll. He shoved the Winchester down
into the saddle boot and tied his saddlebags behind his
saddle.

The sheriff was busy pulling a shoe from each of the
Diamond's horses, including the pack animal they'd used
to bring Reese's body in to town.

When Mike Logan was finished and ready to go he got
the remaining horses out of the stalls, three in all, and
drove them out the back door. This storm wasn't going to
last more than two or three days at the most. The horses
would survive. He said, "If whoever you get to run the
stable for me needs horses, they always bunch up in the
creek bottom down by that old rail fence, or they hang
around out back."

"All right." There was a moment's awkwardness between the two, but the darkness made it less noticeable. Finally Bondy stuck out his hand. "I'm sorry it has to be this way but I know damned well I can't keep you alive if you stay."

Mike was bitter, and angry, but he knew none of this was the sheriff's fault. He stuck out his hand and gripped the sheriff's. "I know." He hesitated a moment and finally said, "Martha ought to be safe enough now. Jasper Diamond isn't going to let any of his other sons bother her after this. I'm going to stop by there but it's late and she may be asleep. Would you mind checking on her every day or two to make sure she's all right?"

Bondy nodded. "Sure I will."

Mike picked up the halter rope of the packhorse. He mounted his saddle horse and rode on out the doors, which Bondy opened for him, into the bitter, horizontal wind. He pulled his hat down as low over his ears as possible so that it would not blow off and turned the collar of his sheepskin up so that it would keep his ears from freezing in the wind.

He did not look back. If Bondy called out anything to him it was instantly snatched away by the wind.

Mike Logan was under no illusions as to what lay ahead of him. For now, the storm and surviving it, no easy task in itself. After that, he would be trailed like a killer wolf, and shot on sight.

There would be Jasper Diamond and his sons. There might also be some of Diamond's crew, because at this time of year most of their ranchwork was done or could at least be postponed.

Two things he knew. He was damned if he was going to leave the country for good, giving up the livery barn, which represented not only his living but everything he'd been able to accumulate so far in his life.

He was also damned if he was going to give up his house. And lastly and most important, he was damned if he was going to give up Martha Lansing.

CHAPTER SIX

There was no way of telling how long this storm was going to last. While it lasted, however dangerous and miserable it might be, Mike Logan would probably be able to stay out of gunshot of Diamond and his sons. But when it cleared . . . The new snow on the ground would make tracking him child's play. The white landscape would make him visible for miles.

He headed north. He wanted to see Martha Lansing once more because he knew it might be a long time before he saw her again. Before he left, he wanted something definite between them, something understood.

He rode north along the street east of that on which stood the Plains Hotel. There wasn't much chance of his being recognized in the snow-swept street by Diamond or by any of his sons in the hotel with him. But if he *was* seen and recognized, they might not only open fire on him but also would know which way he had gone when he left town.

He reached the edge of town and took the road leading north toward Martha Lansing's place. The snow still blew horizontally on a ferocious wind. It still drifted behind everything that broke its force. But it had not yet completely drifted over the tracks of the eight horses on which Diamond and his five sons and the sheriff and his deputy had returned to town.

Mike had no idea where he was going to go. There were ranches scattered over the country north of here, of course, and Mike knew most of those who operated them. But he didn't know any of them well enough to ask them to hide him from Diamond's wrath. Besides that, he felt reasonably sure Diamond would, if he didn't catch him right away, offer a reward. Probably dead or alive. And since few of the ranchers to the north, except for Diamond, did much more than scratch out a difficult living, any reward most certainly would be a temptation to them.

The wind was even more bitterly cold than it had been last time he rode this way. In places, his horses plowed through knee-deep drifts. Mike could feel the cold creeping through his body, making his shoulder ache. He was thoroughly chilled by the time he reached the lane leading to Martha Lansing's house, still visible because of the eight horses' trails.

The house was dark. He hesitated a moment in the lee of it. He was badly chilled and knew he should get warm if he was going to last out the night. On the other hand, he hated waking her, provided, of course, that she was asleep.

His horse decided the issue for him. The animal shook his head and neighed, and almost immediately afterward the faint glow of a lamp lighted one of the windows on this side of the house.

Mike dismounted stiffly and went around to the door.

He knocked lightly and heard Martha's frightened voice on the other side of the door: "Who is it?"

"It's Mike."

The door opened immediately. She was clad in her nightgown, barefooted, with a wrapper around her. Her shining hair was loose, lying on her shoulders. She stepped back away from the blast of wind that carried snow halfway across the room and Mike quickly stepped inside and closed the door behind him. He whispered, "I hope I didn't wake the kids."

She shook her head. "Where are you going at this time of night?"

"Diamond will be after me as soon as it gets light. He intends to kill me for shooting Reese. Says he'll hunt me down like a wolf."

Her face paled and her eyes grew wide. "That's terrible! Can't the sheriff do anything?"

"Not *before* I'm killed. Afterward, he says, he'll arrest Diamond for killing me, but that won't do me much good."

Her eyes were bright with tears. "And you got yourself into this because of me. I'm so sorry, Mike."

"I'm not. I'm just glad I came along when I did." He was. But he knew it might be a long time before he saw her again. There was a chance he wouldn't even survive. There weren't many places to hide in the country around Chimney Rock. He'd have to stay on the move to have any chance at all.

He said, "I've been waiting . . . until it would be a year since your husband died. But I haven't got any more

time to wait. I want you to marry me, Martha. Just as soon
as I get this business finished with."

She didn't pretend surprise. She said, "I knew you were
waiting." She paused a moment, studying his face. Finally
she said, "The children. They're a big responsibility. Not
many men would . . ."

He said, "You know how crazy I am about those kids.
And I think they like me."

She said, "If you're sure . . ."

"I'm sure." He held out his arms and she came naturally
to them even though the front of his coat still was lightly
covered with crusted snow. The shock of touching it
made her start. He released her and she stepped away,
the whole front of her wrapper and gown wet from the
snow. For an instant his eyes were worried as he studied
her face. Then he saw the smile begin in her eyes and an
instant later both of them were laughing.

Mike took off his coat. "Want to try that again?"

She came to him once more, warm and soft. He kissed
her.

He'd kissed her before, but it had never been like this
before. Both gown and wrapper were thin and he could
feel the softness and warmth of her plainly, nearly as
plainly as if neither gown nor wrapper had been there at
all.

He wanted her desperately but this was not the time.
Firmly he pushed her away from him. He said, "Diamond
and his lawyers, if this ever gets to court, will try to make
out that . . ." He paused, wondering how to phrase what
he wanted to say.

But she understood. "I know. Unless you and I have

nothing to hide, we won't sound convincing enough in court."

Mike crossed the room to the stove, standing almost against it, letting its remaining warmth seep through him. Martha asked, "What now? What are you going to do?"

A wry smile touched his mouth. "He said he'd hunt me down like a wolf. I guess I'm supposed to act like a wolf and try to get away."

"In this storm?"

"I'll make it. At least by dawn any tracks I leave will be gone."

Martha looked relieved. "You'll let me know how you are? You'll write?"

"I'll write. Every time I get a chance."

"Have you got food? And everything else you need?"

He said, "I have everything." There were a thousand things he wanted to say to her but there wasn't time for any of them now. He stared steadily at her for a long time, fixing each feature firmly in his memory, almost as if he didn't expect to see her again. Finally he said, "I'm warm now. I've got to go."

She started to protest, but let the protest die on her lips. He shrugged into his coat and buttoned it. "Say goodbye to the kids for me."

"Yes."

"Goodbye." He crossed to the door, then halted with his hand on the bar. She came running across the room and, heedless of the moisture on the front of his coat, flung herself into his arms. "Be careful! Oh, please be careful!"

He nodded. He kissed her lightly, then opened the door

and stepped out into the storm, closing it firmly behind him. He did not hear the bar, so he softly called, "The bar. Keep it in place."

He heard it drop. Pulling on his gloves, he rounded the house toward the place he'd left his horses. He mounted, glanced once at the dim light outlining the window, then rode north along the creek. In a moment everything was lost to his sight and he was riding in a white and screaming void.

───◆───

For several moments Martha Lansing stood at the door, her head on the bar she had just dropped into place. Only moments before she had been gloriously happy, with Mike Logan's strong arms around her, his rough, unshaven cheek against her own. Now she felt a bleak, dismal certainty that she would never see him again. He was riding north in below-zero weather in a wind that could chill a man in minutes no matter how warmly he was dressed. He might lose his way. His horse might fall and break a leg. To make matters worse, he was wounded and had lost a lot of blood.

Angrily she shook herself and crossed the room to the stove. She added wood and put some water into the coffeepot. She couldn't sleep. Not now. So she'd just as well do something to keep her thoughts away from all the terrible things that might happen to Mike.

But her thoughts kept coming back to him. Even if he survived the storm, even if he reached shelter tonight, tomorrow he would be hunted down like a wolf. By Jasper Diamond and his four remaining sons. Later, probably by

Diamond's crewmen too, seven of them in all. Diamond would probably get them all out to hunt for Mike. They'd find him and they'd kill him, and what was worse, if anything could be worse, was that they'd get away with it. Diamond had so much power in the county and in the state that he probably wouldn't even be brought to trial.

But if there was a trial . . . She realized that she was shivering violently. They'd make it sound like she entertained men out here all the time. They'd make it sound like Mike had killed Reese over jealousy, not because Reese was trying to force her against her will.

She made coffee automatically, without realizing what she was doing. She poured a cup, sat down at the table, and drank it with trembling hands, without even tasting it.

Mike was all she could think of, Mike out there, hunted, wounded, and alone. And she was powerless to help. Or was she? Why couldn't she go into town tomorrow and force the sheriff to go out looking for Mike Logan too? If the sheriff and his deputy could find Mike before Diamond did, they could bring him back to town and lodge him in jail, where at least he would be safe.

What if Mike did go to trial? What if they did brand her as a prostitute? Even if Mike was convicted it would be better than having him shot down like a lobo wolf.

But her going to town would depend on the storm, she knew. She didn't dare take her children out in it and she didn't dare leave them alone while she went herself.

At last, as light began to turn the black outside to gray, she finally went back to bed. She was exhausted and she went almost immediately to sleep. But it was an uneasy sleep, from which she awakened often, crying out. However she had to do it, she should have kept Mike Logan here. Now she had lost him. She would never see him again. Fully awake, she began to weep, burying her face in her pillow so that the sounds of her weeping would not awaken the sleeping children.

The wind howled unceasingly in the eaves.

───────◄◆►───────

Sheriff Jack Bondy didn't sleep much better than did Martha Lansing. The cot in the sheriff's office was lumpy and hard. Except for his boots and gunbelt, he was still fully dressed. The stove roared, but in the corner of the room where the cot was, it was cold enough for the sheriff to see his breath.

He shouldn't have let Mike Logan go. He knew that, now that it was too late. Mike was wounded and the storm he was riding into was a killer storm even if a man had all his strength.

And even if Mike, by some miracle, survived the storm, he would still have to contend with Jasper Diamond and his men. Four sons. Seven crewmen. Twelve of them in all; hunting one wounded man who had a start on them of less than half a day.

The storm would probably scour the ground clean of most of the tracks Mike's horses had made. But in places . . . like where the drifts were very deep, there might be enough trail left for them to follow him, particularly if he kept going straight.

And even if they didn't, the storm wasn't going to last. It was only October and this kind of storm was unusual for this time of year. The snow and wind would stop. The sun would come out, blinding upon a white expanse that reached from horizon to horizon. You could see a horse and man for miles in a white landscape like that. And there'd be nothing to hide Mike's trail, once the snow had stopped. There would be no way that he could hide it himself.

The sheriff tossed and turned. Twice he got up and lighted his pipe, stood beside the stove and smoked it. He put more wood into the stove several times. If he got an hour's sleep in all, it was a lot.

He had told Mike he couldn't protect him from Jasper Diamond and his sons. Now he kept asking himself what kind of statement was that for a sheriff to make. What kind of sheriff was he anyway that he'd admit he couldn't protect a prisoner?

Furthermore, he'd told Mike what Jasper Diamond would try doing to Martha Lansing's reputation. The words had not been lies. Diamond *would* try to convince the jury that she was a whore. But a lot of people would testify that she was not. She was respected and well liked in the community.

The bitter truth was—and in these lonely, small hours of the morning, Bondy finally admitted it to himself—sending Mike away had been the simplest way out of a difficult predicament. Simplest for him. Simplest for Martha Lansing. Maybe simplest even for Jasper Diamond and his sons.

But not simplest for Mike. Not fair to Mike. Because Mike was probably going to give his life for doing what any decent man would have done in the same circumstances. And at the moment, Bondy didn't see what he could do to change the situation that had been caused by his advice to Mike.

CHAPTER SEVEN

As Mike Logan headed north into the howling blast of snow-laden wind, he tried to decide, and quickly, what he was going to do.

If he was to survive the storm, he had to have two things: shelter for himself and feed for his horses. The horses would be able to stand a lot of cold but only if they had their bellies full.

Mike searched his memory for a place that would provide both things. Desperately he tried to recall if there were any abandoned ranches where the buildings, however ramshackle, would provide him the shelter he had to have, where exposed grassland would be scoured clean of snow and would provide feed for his horses.

He could think of no such place, at least none that wasn't occupied. But he did remember something—a bluff whose lee side was on the south and would provide shelter from the wind. On top of the bluff was a flat expanse of grass that the wind would probably have kept scoured clean.

It was more than fifteen miles away. Too far to ride in

this savage gale. Too long to be exposed to the bitter cold.
But there wasn't any other choice.

Before he had gone ten miles in the direction of the
bluff, his hands were completely numb. Awkwardly, he
wrapped the reins of his saddle horse around his left
wrist. He wound the lead rope of the packhorse around
the saddlehorn and tucked the end between his leg and
the saddle. He knew he couldn't tie a knot. Not now. His
hands were just too cold.

His feet felt like stumps. He tried to wriggle his toes
and discovered that he could not.

Would he freeze to death out here? Maybe that was
what Jasper Diamond really wanted. If he froze to death,
Diamond would be relieved of the need to kill him. He
could have his vengeance without the risk of being
brought to trial.

Mike shook his head. No. Diamond didn't want that
kind of impersonal vengeance. He wanted to kill Mike
with his own two hands.

Mike kicked his horse in the ribs to try making him go
a little faster. The horse broke into a trot.

He began to feel drowsy. His head drooped forward
and his eyes closed. He felt himself slipping away.

Frantically he snapped himself upright. He shook his
head, trying to clear it. Falling asleep was the worst thing
he could do right now. If he went to sleep he would probably not awaken. He would fall from his horse and die in
the snow. By morning his body would be stiff as a board.

Alternately he slapped his hands against his chap-clad
legs. They hurt ferociously each time they struck his legs.
His wounded shoulder began to throb with pain from the

movement of his arm. But the pain made his drowsiness disappear.

And the slapping action of his hands against his legs must have made the circulation improve in his hands because they too began to hurt. He thought ironically that even though he had plenty of matches on his packhorse, he might not be able to use them when he reached the bluff. His hands might be too stiff to build a fire or strike a match.

He began slapping them against his thighs more vigorously. He had been following the creek that wound past Martha Lansing's house. Now, believing he was close, he began to look for the place it forked, knowing he had to follow the right-hand fork to reach the bluff.

He could scarcely see the ground. Trees and brush appeared only occasionally. Sometimes they were seen only when either he or one of the horses brushed against them, dislodging the snow with which they were crusted and nearly concealed.

Slowly, slowly, a dismal certainty began to creep over Mike. He wasn't going to find the bluff. He was either going to ride past it in the storm or he was going to freeze to death sitting in his saddle before he ever got that far.

But he was stubborn and he was tough. There was an implacable will to live in him. So when his mind grew dull from drowsiness, he deliberately induced pain in his shoulder or in his hands and feet to snap him out of his lethargy. He reached the fork in the stream, recognizing it when his horses went down into the left-hand branch and climbed out on the other side. Bearing right, he also felt it when they crossed the right-hand fork.

Half an hour later he saw the bluff, rising ghostly and dark before his eyes. He rode straight to the foot of it before he stopped.

Now would come the test. Dismounting—the simple act of getting off his horse—was going to be one of the hardest things he had ever done. Once off, he would have to move around sufficiently to restore the circulation to his half-frozen limbs.

Then he had to find and gather wood. He had to clear a spot of snow and carefully pile twigs in the form of a tepee so that they would catch from a lighted match.

Fortunately, the wood he would find wasn't likely to be wet. The air had turned bitter cold at the same time the snow had begun, so none had melted and therefore the snow would not have soaked anything.

His two horses crowded up close to the rock wall, grateful to be out of the wind. Mike made himself move, made himself go through the motions of dismounting.

He succeeded in part. He got his right leg over the horse's rump and swung it toward the ground.

Touching the ground, it gave way under him. He fell, his left foot still caught in the stirrup.

Normally this would have frightened the horse and he might have run. But the horse was also cold. He stood motionless while Mike pulled himself up, trying laboriously to free the foot, which might not have caught at all except for the overshoe.

Gloomily he thought that maybe this was the way he was going to die. He wouldn't be able to free the foot and he'd hang here until he froze.

Then suddenly his foot came free, slipping out of the

overshoe, which then itself fell to the ground. Mike crawled through the snow to the wall of the bluff. He pulled himself upright with the help of a three-foot boulder lying on the ground.

There was excruciating pain in both feet and both hands. His shoulder felt as if there were a fire burning there. He forced his mind to function. Wood, he thought. And he stumbled away into the void, sliding his feet back and forth so that any wood lying loose would be dislodged and could be picked up.

How long this went on he had no idea. But finally he had a small armload of wood and headed back toward the horses, waiting patiently where he had left them at the foot of the bluff.

He laid the wood down carefully in a spot he first cleared by kicking a boot back and forth in the snow. He went to his packhorse and fumbled with hands that had no feeling for the matches he knew he had brought.

He found them finally and got a small handful of them. He returned to his firewood after slipping the matches beneath the flap of his sheepskin and into the pocket of his shirt, where they would stay dry.

Laboriously, kneeling in the snow, he selected the smallest of the twigs. He built himself a small pyramid. Time lost meaning. He didn't know whether it took him five minutes or fifty. What he did know was that if he did not get this fire started, he was going to die. Diamond would find him lying here, his body solid ice.

So he forced himself not to hurry, to work only slowly and deliberately so that the job would be done right the first time and would not have to be redone.

The minutes fled swiftly past. The horses stood patiently, glad to be out of the wind. Mike thought bleakly that if the matches were the least bit wet . . . if the wind blew out their flame before the twigs he had so carefully arranged caught from it . . . if the wood was too wet to burn . . . If any of these possibilities became reality, then he was dead. But all he could do was try. As long as the spark of life remained.

———◆———

Jasper Diamond was up before dawn. The fire in the stove in the center of his room had gone out but he didn't bother to light another one. He could see his breath nearly halfway across the room. He dressed quickly, shivering, putting on his overshoes over his boots and slipping into his sheepskin coat. He tied a bandanna over his head to cover his ears before cramming on his battered, wide-brimmed hat. As soon as he was completely dressed, he went along the hall, banging on his sons' doors until he heard each of them up and moving around. To each he yelled, "I'll be down in the kitchen rounding up some grub. Meet me there. And hurry up. We want to get out of here as soon as it gets light."

There were a few sleepily protesting voices over the noise at this hour of the morning but Diamond characteristically ignored them. He clumped noisily down the stairs to the kitchen of the hotel.

Jess Gorgen and his Chinese helper, Ling, were already there. Ling was building a fire in the stove. Jess was putting on the coffeepot. Diamond said, "Get a couple of gunnysacks, Jess. Put in enough grub for five men for about a week. And some cooking pots and eatin' tools."

Jess started to open his mouth, then closed it without saying anything after one look at Diamond's face. He immediately went out into the yard behind the hotel where there was a shed for coal and wood. He came back with several gunnysacks, which he proceeded to fill. By the time he had finished, the fire in the stove was roaring, the coffeepot was boiling, and Diamond's four remaining sons had arrived, some of them still putting on their outer clothing.

Diamond said, "Get yourselves some coffee and biscuits. But make it fast. He's probably got a good start on us."

The sons—all of them big, all grown men—each got a coffee cup and filled it. They sat down at the table and began wolfing down stale biscuits liberally spread with marmalade from a gallon jar. Diamond gave them ten minutes. Then he said harshly, "That's enough. Let's go. Each of you grab one of those sacks."

He went out the back door without even bothering to thank Jess and Ling, and his sons followed him. First came Lentz, looking a lot like Diamond himself must have looked in his younger days. Hank followed Lentz. Then came Hugo and last came Rudy, now the youngest since the old man's favorite, Reese, was dead.

They went down the alley single file, cut through a vacant lot, and hit the main street, forced to lean into the wind as the full force of it struck them. Rudy's hat blew off and went rolling down the street, with Rudy in pursuit. He didn't catch up with the hat until he was right in front of the livery stable.

The five went inside. The minute he saw the horses, Diamond scowled suspiciously. If he'd been Mike Logan, he wouldn't have left the six Diamond horses for them to chase him on. Then he looked down at their feet. Each was missing a shoe. They could be ridden, but not in pursuit of Mike Logan. Not without all of their shoes. He could go back home and get fresh horses but that would take time he didn't have. To Lentz he said, "Find Logan's horse-shoeing nails. I'm goin' to get Bondy and find out what he did with those shoes."

He marched down the street to the jail and banged inside. Bondy was still asleep on the cot. Diamond went over to it and yanked the covers off. He said, "Get up and get dressed, you sonofabitch, and come down to the livery barn. I want those horseshoes and I want them now."

Bondy said sleepily, "I don't know . . ."

Diamond withdrew his gun. He cocked it and shoved it against Bondy's chest. "You got half a minute to change your mind."

Bondy stared up into his face a moment. His expression said he knew Diamond had been pushed as far as he was going to be. He wanted Mike Logan and he wasn't going to let anything stand in his way.

Bondy shrugged. "All right. They're in the snowbank on the south side of the livery barn. About three feet back from the corner."

"They'd better be where you say they are." Angrily, Diamond stamped outside, slamming the door so hard the windows rattled.

He hurried down to the stable, rounded the corner on the downwind side, and three feet from the corner dug down into the snow. He was immediately rewarded when his hand encountered something hard. One by one he uncovered the six shoes. He carried them into the livery stable and threw them down on the floor. "Put them back on. Be sure you get the right shoes on the right horses."

Lentz lifted one of the horse's feet and tried each shoe until he found the one that fit. Swiftly and efficiently, he nailed it on. He followed the same procedure with the other horses and in half an hour the job was done.

Diamond led out into the street, still bleak and snow-swept with not, at this hour, a living soul in sight. The only smoke came from the chimney at the jail.

Jasper Diamond knew this was going to be a long, hard chase, particularly if the snow kept up. Even if the sky cleared, the wind would continue and there would be little change in conditions near the ground. Snow would continue blowing, cutting visibility to a few hundred yards, or sometimes feet.

Catching Mike Logan was going to be more than a simple chase, more than tracking him. He was going to have to outthink Mike Logan if he ever intended to catch the man.

Taking one shoe off each Diamond horse had been smart, even if it hadn't worked. Leaving in the middle of the night also had been smart, ensuring that there would be no trail to follow when it got light.

But Mike Logan had to have some place to go. Frowning, Diamond considered where that might be.

Several ranchers lived north of town, and all of them were beholden to Diamond in one way or another, for graze in years when grass was scarce, for small cash loans, for orphaned calves, which Diamond had no time for but which could be bottle raised. Logan would hardly risk going to one of them for help.

But he had to have shelter from this bitter gale and he had to have some kind of feed for his horses. Diamond's mind went instantly to the bluff, just as Mike's had done. The bluff would provide shelter from the wind. The top of it would be scoured clean and there would be grass for the horses there.

Cautiously, he reviewed his decision as to where Mike would go. Hell, he thought, the bluff was the only place Mike *could* go.

He suddenly felt a little sorry that this was going to end so soon. He had told Mike he would hunt him down like a wolf and that was what he meant to do. But it ought to last longer than a day. He wanted Mike to run, to be scared, to have time to regret the killing of Reese, Diamond's youngest son. He wanted Mike exhausted, half frozen, a broken man when he finally was killed.

A mile out of town they encountered three crewmen riding in. One was Sandy Price, another Harrison. Sturges was the third. Diamond yelled at them over the howling wind to fall in behind.

CHAPTER EIGHT

Mike Logan finished building the fire framework in the best way he could. Snow had sifted down and dusted it lightly, and that snow would melt as soon as there was any heat from beneath, but by that time the fire would probably have a start.

He stuck his ungloved hands inside his coat for several shivering minutes, trying to get them warm enough to strike a match. They began to hurt ferociously as they warmed up, but he kept clenching and unclenching them underneath his coat until he judged they were warm enough to function.

Taking one hand out, he picked up a rock he had previously uncovered and blew the snow off it. With his right hand he selected a match from among those in his shirt pocket, and by feel got hold of the right end.

Tense with worry, he brought the match out and quickly struck it against the semidry surface of the rock. Nothing happened. Frantically he struck it again, and this time it caught. But before he could get it beneath his little tepee of sticks, the wind snuffed it out. Logan cursed.

There was a cold knot of fear growing in him now. If he failed to light this fire he knew he would not survive.

He returned both hands to the inside of his coat, and clamped each one between an arm and his body. Because his legs were going numb in a crouched position, he got up and paced nervously back and forth, waiting for his hands to warm again.

When he felt the circulation return to his fingers he went back to the wood he had so carefully piled up and knelt beside it again. Once more he located his striking rock and wiped its surface off against a place on his sleeve. With his other hand, he selected another match from his shirt pocket, fumbled with it until he had hold of the right end, then prepared to bring it out.

This time, he crouched over the pile of sticks, his back to the wind, his arms and shoulders helping to provide a shield. He brought out the match and quickly and firmly struck it against the rock. It flared, sputtered once, then flamed the way it should.

With a hand that trembled violently, both from cold and nervousness, he pushed it underneath his little tepee of sticks. Touching one of the sticks, he dislodged it and for an instant thought the whole thing would come tumbling down. But it only settled slightly, and a moment later one stick caught, then another, then another still. He waited there, crouched to protect the tiny blaze, until it had begun to burn some of the larger sticks. Then, carefully, he got to his feet.

With the wind now fanning the flame, the fire was growing rapidly. Mike immediately began to search for more fuel, kicking around in the snow at the foot of the bluff.

He found a few small sticks. He also found a limb of a piñon tree that had evidently been dead a long time and had probably been broken off its parent tree by the wind. He knew it was loaded with pitch and would burn a long time with a very hot flame.

He returned to the fire and added to it the smaller sticks he had picked up. Then, bracing the branch against the wall of the bluff, he kicked it firmly. Being brittle because it was so dry, it broke in two. He began breaking the two pieces into smaller ones until he had two large armloads of wood.

The exertion had warmed him, but hands, feet, and wounded shoulder still ached terribly. Carefully he added some of his pitchy wood to the now-blazing fire and crouched over it so close that his wet coat began immediately to steam.

The fire illuminated the wall of the bluff. Snow, melting and then hitting the blazing sticks, made a slight hissing sound.

Mike began to get warm again. When his front was warmed, he stood and put his back to the fire, turning himself like a piece of meat being barbecued so that neither side got too warm, neither side too cold.

Finally, when he felt a bit more comfortable, he went to his packhorse and got some cold meat and crackers from the pack. He also got the coffeepot, some coffee, and a cup.

He filled the pot with melted snow and held it over the blaze, occasionally adding more snow. When he had the pot half filled with hot water, he added some coffee, permitted it to boil a few moments, then set it aside to settle the grounds. While he waited, he finished the crackers and meat, and when the coffee was ready, poured himself a cup. Finishing that quickly, he poured another and again quickly drank the body-warming brew. Finishing what little coffee was left, he dumped out the grounds, cleaned pot and cup with snow, then put them away.

He was pleasantly surprised at how well he felt. It still was cold, but the deadly chill had gone from his body and from his extremities.

It had been light for some time, a gray and gloomy light. He had better start thinking about his horses, he realized.

He knelt and warmed himself for one last time over the glowing coals of the fire. Then he scattered it with a boot, making sure that every ember was out. He didn't want to provide Diamond and his men with a ready-made fire. Let them do it the hard way, just as he had.

He picked up the reins of the packhorse and mounted his saddle horse. Slipping on his now-dry gloves, he rode along the face of the bluff until he reached a break in it. He put his horse onto a steep trail leading up.

He reached the top. He tied up the reins of his saddle horse, took the bit out of his mouth, then staked him out where the ground had been swept bare by the hard driving wind. He tied up the packhorse's halter rope but didn't bother staking him out, knowing he would stay with the saddle horse.

Both horses immediately put their rumps to the wind and began to graze. Taking his rifle out of the saddle boot and getting a pocketful of ammunition for it from the pack, Mike returned to the edge of the bluff.

He climbed down six or eight feet into a small pocket between two rocks. There was a little shelter from the wind here. Hunching down into his coat, putting his gloved hands into the coat pockets, he braced his back against one of the rocks and stared into the blowing snow, waiting for his pursuers to appear. He had little faith that Bondy's removal of a shoe from each of their horses would slow them much.

They'd be almost on him, he thought, before he glimpsed them at all. Briefly he considered the possibility that they'd try to come on him from the rear, from the top of the plateau. He discarded that notion immediately. They were going to have as hard a time as he had locating the bluff in the driving snow. They wouldn't risk missing it altogether by attempting to circle it and come on him from behind.

The entire sky by now was a lighter gray. Once, briefly, the snow cleared immediately over Mike's head and he glimpsed blue sky.

So it was a ground blizzard now. The sky had cleared and the snow was no longer coming down. But the ferocious wind, which had not diminished at all, was blowing the snow already on the ground, creating blizzard conditions for fifty to a hundred feet above the ground.

The clear sky offered Mike no immediate relief either from the lack of visibility or from the cold. But it did warn him that soon, perhaps today, the wind would die. The air would warm. The sun would shine upon the ground. When those things happened, his trail from then on would be plain and easily followed by anyone. There would be no hiding it in the vast expanse of snow that lay all about him.

So now, here, he had to slow Jasper Diamond or make him turn back if he could. He checked the rifle to be sure of its loads. He arranged his coat so that his right hand would have instant access to his extra rifle ammunition. And he waited.

Twice more in the next couple of hours he briefly glimpsed blue sky overhead. And at last he caught a glimpse of dark moving shapes coming through the curtain of snow at the foot of the bluff.

Instantly his body tensed. He brought the rifle into a ready position and thumbed the hammer back. Wait, he thought, until you can be sure.

The shapes materialized more clearly as they came into the area on the lee side of the bluff, where there was little wind. Mike counted them. Jasper Diamond was unmistakable because of his size. Mike thought he recognized at least three of Diamond's sons, although all four were probably along. The others were probably members of Diamond's crew.

During the war Mike had fired at human beings, but he hadn't done it since. He carefully drew a bead on Jasper Diamond. But he couldn't shoot. It was too cold-blooded.

He changed his point of aim and squeezed off the trigger. Diamond's horse reared, dumping Diamond from his saddle into the snow. Mike changed his point of aim again, once more trying to hit a horse instead of a man. He saw horse and man go down. He saw the man get up and hop away, bending, holding his leg with both hands.

He took only half a dozen hops before he sprawled face downward in the snow.

Diamond's horse was down and kicking. The other horse was still. One man began firing at Mike from the back of his prancing horse. Mike paid no attention to him. The others were milling, and in another instant they would all gallop out of range. Mike took aim at still another horse and fired quickly.

He knew, even as he squeezed off the trigger, that he had missed the horse. He had shot too high. But just as he fired, the horse's rider spurred him. The horse surged forward enough that the rider got the bullet intended for the horse. He tumbled from the saddle and lay completely still. Mike knew with a sinking feeling that he had hit the man in the chest and that the man almost certainly was dead.

Diamond was up on his feet, rifle in hands, firing at the top of the bluff. Mike returned the fire, aiming at horses, and he downed one more and nicked a fourth in the chest just enough to sting the animal and make him rear.

Mike realized that they couldn't see him. In the blowing snow, he must blend enough with the rocks to make him invisible to those below.

And then the men below him broke. Those who were afoot ran. Those who still had horses galloped away into the concealment of the blowing snow. They left behind two dead horses and one still kicking but unable to get up. They dragged the dead man but carried the man Mike had shot in the leg. And suddenly everything was still.

Mike knew it was time for him to go. He scrambled

back to the top of the bluff. He pulled the stake securing his saddle horse, coiled the rope, and, holding the halter rope of his packhorse, mounted and headed north.

He had killed a man and had probably crippled another one. He felt depressed. But he knew he'd had no choice. Diamond wasn't given to idle threats, and he had said he would hunt him down and kill him like a wolf.

He rode away, knowing the wind and drifting snow still would hide his trail. But no longer did he need the same things he had needed when he left Chimney Rock. He needed no shelter and he needed no special place where he could find feed for his horses, because he knew the storm was going to clear.

He *could* just keep riding north, leaving behind his livery stable and his house. That way, he might escape Diamond's vengeful wrath. But he could never send for Martha because Diamond would follow her.

The price of his life, then, was everything he had worked for all these years and the woman he loved. To hell with Jasper Diamond. It was too high a price to pay.

He would run for a while, fighting back when they caught up with him and he was forced to fight to save his life. But he wouldn't give up everything. He wouldn't leave the country for good.

If Diamond persisted in hunting him down like an animal, then Diamond was going to have to pay the price. The way he had today.

CHAPTER NINE

Jasper Diamond had never been quite so furious in his entire life. He was, in the first place, almost numb with cold. He was sick with grief over the death of his son Reese, who, he was convinced, had been murdered over a woman whose favors were probably for sale to anyone who had the price. Mike had caught them together and in his fury had pursued and killed Reese. Mike might have believed Martha Lansing to be virtuous. In any case, it didn't matter anymore. Reese was lying on a slab at Halliburton's, awaiting burial as soon as the weather moderated. And sooner or later, one way or another, Mike Logan was going to die for killing him. Now, he had been ambushed. Lentz had been shot in the leg. One of his crewmen had been killed. He had lost three horses and, he knew, had also lost Mike by now. Mike would have wasted no time riding away from the scene of the ambush, and with the wind blowing the way it was, by the time Diamond got around to looking for Mike's tracks, they would have been wiped out.

His men had retreated a couple of hundred yards, far enough from the bluff to be concealed by the snow from

Logan, who had been firing from the top. Lentz was on the ground, two of his brothers kneeling at his side. The dead man was Sandy Price, short, bowlegged, skinny, and middle-aged, who had been with Jasper Diamond almost a dozen years.

Diamond felt bad about Price but he didn't waste time with him as soon as he had ascertained that he was dead. He hurried to his son, seeing the spreading stain of red beneath Lentz's right knee.

Hank and Rudy had already cut away Lentz's pants and underwear to expose the wound.

It was a nasty one. White bone splinters were visible in the shredded flesh. The bleeding was massive. Diamond bawled, "Anybody got whiskey?"

One of the crewmen dug a brown bottle out of a saddlebag and brought it to him. Diamond yelled, "Mufflers! Anybody got mufflers?" He had one himself, wrapped twice around his neck so that he could pull it up to cover his face and protect it against the icy wind. He knelt and wrapped his own muffler around Lentz's knee. It was almost instantly soaked with blood. He snatched one after another from the men, wrapping them around the knee similarly. When he had four wrapped around the knee and tied, he emptied the bottle of whiskey over the whole thing.

Lentz was unconscious but his chest still rose and fell. Diamond yelled over the howling wind, "He can't ride! Tie him over one of the saddles. The rest of you double up. Put Price over the rump of one of your horses and tie him down. Hurry, damn it!"

The men moved swiftly. Lentz was laid over a saddle

and tied in place. His left leg was tied with a rope passed beneath the horse's belly, his wounded leg tied to the unhurt leg with another muffler, so that it wouldn't flop around.

Ten minutes after the shooting, they were on their way back to town. Diamond and his son Hank rode on one horse. Rudy rode with Hugo, leading Lentz's horse. Harrison and Sturges had doubled up, thus making up for the third horse Mike had shot.

Before the shooting, Diamond had been chilled to the bone. Now there was a different kind of coldness inside of him. He had lost Reese. Lentz, if he lived, would probably lose his right leg above the knee and would therefore be a cripple the rest of his life. Sandy Price, for whom Jasper Diamond had felt a genuine affection, was dead. Most infuriating of all was the fact that Mike Logan had escaped without a scratch.

Diamond rode in the lead, setting as fast a pace as he dared. He followed their own trail back along the creek until he reached the fork. Then he cut left, knowing he would shortly hit the road.

He did. Most of the tracks they'd made previously had drifted over, but enough unevenness was left to see. The horses plowed through knee-deep snow much of the way, lunging, and several times Diamond wondered how Lentz could possibly reach town alive, the way his body was being thrown back and forth by the horse's movements. But there was no help for it. If Lentz didn't get to the doctor, he was going to bleed to death, if he hadn't already done so.

There were a few people on the streets when they rode

into town. The wind seemed to have moderated. Occasionally Diamond would see a small patch of blue sky overhead, which told him the snow had stopped and that what now remained was a ground blizzard, which would stop as soon as the wind died down.

He followed Lentz's horse, which Rudy and Hugo were leading, straight to Dr. Eggleston's house. He told the other men he'd meet them later in the Pink Lady Saloon.

Dr. Eggleston lived in a big two-story white frame house a couple of blocks north of the business section of the town. As soon as they reached the front gate, Diamond bawled, "Doc! Eggleston! My boy's been shot!"

The door opened. Already Hugo and Rudy were busy untying Lentz from the saddle of his horse. They carried him in, with Jasper Diamond and Hank following, steadying Lentz's leg as best they could. Doc met them at the door, stout, white-haired, a little florid in the face. Doc drank a lot but it never seemed to affect the way he did his job.

Diamond didn't even know whether Lentz was still alive as Hugo and Rudy carried him into an adjoining room and laid him on the high, flat operating table there. Doc unbuttoned Lentz's coat and shirt and underwear with swift fingers and put a stethoscope to his chest. He grunted. "Alive, but just barely so. Get out of here and tell my wife to come in." He was busily unwinding the many mufflers Diamond had tied around Lentz's knee in the hope of preventing him from bleeding to death.

Diamond retreated, calling for Mrs. Eggleston. She hurried from the kitchen, disappeared into the operating room, and closed the door. Half frozen, Jasper Diamond and his three sons hunched over the stove in the center of Eggleston's parlor, shivering and listening.

It seemed like hours before the door opened and Eggleston stuck his head out. "I can't save the leg. I ain't sure I can save him. You want me to amputate?"

Diamond said harshly, "Do what you got to do, Doc. But save his life, you hear?"

"I'll do my best." Doc withdrew.

Another eternity of waiting. A couple of times the sun came out, but it disappeared almost immediately again. Diamond let himself think of Mike Logan. Maybe Logan didn't know it yet, but he was a dead man. Everything else on the Diamond Ranch was going to stop until he was caught and killed.

An hour after they had brought Lentz in, Doc Eggleston finally opened the door. He was wiping his hands on a towel. He wore a white apron, the front of which was red with blood. "I took his leg above the knee. He's alive, but . . . well, I just don't know. Another man would've been dead by now."

Diamond nodded and got to his feet. He had things to do. He looked at Rudy. "You stay. I want to know—if he dies—or if Doc says he's goin' to make it."

"Sure, pa."

Diamond gestured toward Hugo and Hank with a jerk of his head. The three went out. Diamond mounted the horse he had ridden here. Hugo mounted the one he had shared with Rudy. Hank mounted the one across which Lentz had been tied.

Diamond led the way down the street the two blocks to the Pink Lady Saloon. The wind had moderated and he could see the sun dimly through the blowing snow. Enough wind was left, though, for what he had in mind.

He didn't even dismount in front of the saloon. To Hugo he said, "Go get 'em."

Hugo went in and a few moments later came out, the two crew members following. With himself, thought Diamond, that made five. Enough to hunt Mike Logan down. Enough, too, for something else he intended to do before he left town.

The men mounted, afterward buttoning coats and turning collars up against the wind. Diamond thought that if it stayed clear tonight, which it likely would, the temperature might go to twenty below. But it wouldn't be so bad if there was no wind.

He rode down the street toward the livery barn. The sheriff came out of his office and stood on the walk, hands on hips, staring at them as they went by. Diamond didn't stop.

He led his little cavalcade into the livery barn. He said, "Hugo, go up in the layloft. Drop a match in a loose pile of hay, then get the hell down here as fast as you can. We're going to burn his house too and I don't want the sheriff butting in."

Hugo obediently climbed the ladder to the loft. He was back down almost immediately. Diamond asked, "You're sure it caught?"

"It caught." Diamond glanced up and saw smoke billowing across the opening through which the ladder went.

Satisfied, he rode down the ramp and into the street, turned quickly, and headed for Mike Logan's small house.

There wasn't any hay there and it might be hard to make the house burn, so he said to Hank, "Go down to Seward's Store. Get a can of coal oil. Hurry up. In a minute the goddamn fire bell is going to ring."

Hank galloped away. Diamond led those who remained straight to Mike Logan's house. The door wasn't locked. He went inside and looked around.

It was a bachelor's place, that was obvious at a glance. Untidy. Plain. The ashes needed taking out and there were dirty dishes in the sink. Distantly, dimmed by the walls of the house, Diamond heard the fire bell. A few moments later, Hank came in, carrying a gallon can of coal oil with a potato over its spout. Diamond took it from him. He went into the bedroom and poured coal oil liberally over Mike's bed. He poured a trail out into the parlor and liberally doused the furniture. He lighted a match, threw it on the bed, and watched the flames grow. In seconds the whole upper half of the house was filled with a dense cloud of black smoke. Diamond said, "Break out the windows and open both the doors. Then let's go."

With chairs, his men broke the windows out. Someone opened the back door and they all trooped out the front. The firebell was ringing more insistently now, and Diamond could see the column of smoke rising from the livery barn. Every now and then when the wind slackened momentarily, he could see flames above the houses in between.

He led his sons and crew out of town, headed home. They'd get fresh horses and pick up the remaining members of his crew.

Diamond left town without going near the main street,

where all the people had gathered. But he sent Harrison to the saloon to pass the word that he'd pay five hundred dollars for Logan, dead or alive. There was some small satisfaction in him now. He had hurt Mike Logan. Not as much as Logan had hurt him, but some. And even if the reward didn't work, maybe he'd stirred him up enough to make him come to those pursuing him.

But he wouldn't count on that. He'd told Mike Logan he'd hunt him down like a wolf and that was what he meant to do.

Jack Bondy watched Jasper Diamond, his sons Hank and Hugo, and his two crew members ride down the street toward the livery barn. He knew about Lentz being shot. He knew that Sandy Price was dead. Nobody had told him any details, but he supposed they had caught up with Mike and that Mike had fought back successfully.

Later, there might be a charge of murder lodged against Mike, but Bondy doubted he would live long enough to face a trial.

He went back inside his office, thinking that Diamond and his men were only going to the stable for fresh mounts. Then he remembered. There weren't any fresh mounts there. He and Mike had turned all the horses out.

He whirled and ran for the door, in time to see smoke billowing out of the wide front doors, which Diamond had left open.

Bondy sprinted for the church. The bell tower was reached by a stairway, the door to which was never locked. Bondy ran up the stairs and frantically began to ring the bell, which, on every day but Sunday, was considered to be the town's fire bell. People poured into the streets.

Even as they did, Bondy knew it was no use. In this wind, that stable didn't have the chance of a snowball in hell. Fortunately, there was nothing close enough to catch on the lee side of it. A few people down there watching for sparks landing on other roofs would be about all that was needed.

From the tower, he saw Hank Diamond come out of Seward's Store carrying a coal-oil can. Bondy knew what that was for. He stopped ringing the bell and ran down the stairs. One of the town kids, a boy of about fourteen, was running past. Bondy yelled, "Ring the bell! Keep ringing it!" and headed for Mike Logan's house.

While he was still half a block away, he knew it was no use. Black oily smoke poured out of the broken windows and the open doors. The most anyone could do was see to it that the fire didn't spread.

Bondy returned to the main street, where most of the people were. He directed half a dozen to Mike Logan's house, instructing them to draw water from Logan's well and see to it that the houses downwind from Logan's house didn't catch.

With bitter anger then, he watched as the flames consumed the livery barn. Mike Logan was wiped out and in danger of losing his life. And only because he had done what any decent man would do. He had tried to protect Martha Lansing from Reese Diamond.

Maybe he hadn't had to pursue Reese out into the snow. But Bondy couldn't blame him because he had. He'd probably have done the same damn thing himself.

Well, tomorrow, if the weather cleared, he'd do what he could. He'd arrest Jasper Diamond and charge him with arson in the burning of Mike's house and the livery barn. With Jasper Diamond in jail, maybe this insanity would stop. Then he remembered the coal-oil can he had seen Hank Diamond carrying from Seward's Store.

He got up and reached for his coat and hat. He wasn't going to give up. Maybe he didn't have any evidence yet to throw Jasper Diamond in jail. But he had enough to take Hank. And that would decrease the odds against Mike Logan by one. It wasn't much, but maybe it would help.

CHAPTER TEN

After the shooting at the bluff, Mike waited. He could hear Diamond down below, shouting. Finally there was only silence. He guessed they had withdrawn and had gone back to town.

He knew he had downed three horses. He was fairly sure that, without meaning to, he had killed one man. And he knew he had wounded another man in the leg. He guessed, and rightly, that the wounded man was one of Jasper Diamond's sons. Otherwise Diamond would never have given up the pursuit.

Satisfied that they were gone, he climbed to where his horses were. He mounted and rode north immediately. He occasionally glimpsed blue sky overhead. But the ground blizzard still obscured visibility.

It had been several hours since Mike had put out his fire and by now he was chilled thoroughly again. The sun did not get through the blowing snow close to the ground, and so had no warming effect. Furthermore, Mike knew, because of the clear sky, that when night fell the temperature was going to plunge maybe to fifteen or twenty below.

He might get through the day without freezing his hands and feet, though it was doubtful. He wouldn't get through the night. He needed help if he was going to stay alive. He needed help today, and he needed help tonight. In his mind he went over the ranches nearest to where he was right now. Rafael Castillo's place was closest and he felt he could count on Rafael to give him sanctuary. Rafael's wife would feed him and he could warm himself thoroughly there, feeling safe.

The trouble was, if Jasper Diamond found out that Castillo had given him sanctuary, then Rafael would be subject to Diamond's reprisals and Rafael's situation was already precarious enough.

Who else? Well, there was Lester Egan. Mike didn't like Egan much, but that didn't have much to do with the situation in which he now found himself. He wouldn't dare sleep at Egan's because he knew he couldn't trust the man. But he could go there and get warm. He could get hot food. And if he was thoroughly warm and well fed when he left, he could get through the rest of the day. He'd worry about the coming night later on.

He turned his horses, heading back toward Egan's place, between Diamond's place and town, hoping the ground blizzard would thin occasionally as he traveled so that he could see the landmarks he needed to find Egan's place.

He supposed that, by now, it was afternoon. Once, in the lee of a low bluff that he recognized as being on a direct route to Egan's place, he dismounted, stamped his feet, flailed his arms, and paced rapidly back and forth long enough to get the circulation going again. After that, he rummaged in the gunnysack tied to the packsaddle and found a few dry biscuits to eat. He continued to pace while he finished eating them, then reluctantly got back onto his horse and headed for Egan's place again.

Several more times blue sky showed through the blowing snow. The wind began to die. Landmarks became visible more frequently. The sun settled toward the horizon.

Under normal conditions, Mike would have reached Egan's place long before sundown. But he had done some wandering, looking for landmarks in the storm. His horses were weary from floundering around in drifts. He'd had to travel across country, there being no road between the bluff and Egan's place.

Egan's spread consisted of a small, three-room house, a log barn, several smaller buildings, and the soddy that had been the Egans' original dwelling when they settled here ten years ago.

Riding in, Mike fumbled with chilled hands until he found his revolver. He withdrew it from its holster and stuck it down into the side pocket of his coat. He rode his horses straight to Egan's barn, dismounted, and opened the door and led them inside. A dog came from somewhere to bark at him but there was no sign of activity at the house.

Inside the barn, Mike found hay for his horses and forked them a pile of it. He tied up the packhorse's halter rope, removing the bit from his saddle horse's mouth without entirely removing the bridle because he knew he might have to leave here fast.

Leaving the horses eating hay, he opened the door again and headed for the house, the dog yelping at his heels. He cursed the dog mildly, and the dog, hearing words he recognized, stopped barking.

Egan himself opened the back door. Mike went in when he stood aside. "Hello, Les. Some storm, isn't it?"

Egan stared at him. "What are you doing here? If Diamond should find out . . ."

"How's Diamond going to find out? He can't track me in this storm. All I need is a chance to get warm and some hot food."

He crossed the room without removing his sheepskin coat and got as close as he could to the kitchen range. Mrs. Egan, thin and wrinkled, but strong enough to do both her work around the house and the chores outside, said, "I ain't got much to give you, but we had chicken for supper and I got some left."

Mike said, "I'd appreciate it, Mrs. Egan." He moved slightly to one side so that she could reach the stove.

Egan kept staring at him, nervous speculation in his eyes. Mrs. Egan asked, "You want some coffee now?"

"Yes, ma'am. That would sure go good."

She poured him a cup. He held it in his right hand as he sipped it appreciatively. He wondered briefly how Egan had known Diamond was hunting him, then decided Egan must have been to town.

He drank about half the coffee and started to put down the cup. Glancing up, he saw that Egan had a rifle in his hands. The man looked scared as he jacked a cartridge into the chamber of the gun. "Hold it, Logan. Hold it right where you are. Don't try getting under that coat for your gun."

Logan shrugged. "All right. You doing Diamond's dirty

work for him now?" The coffee cup was in his right hand, so there wasn't much use thinking about the gun in the pocket of his coat. Besides, Egan could shoot him long before he could get it out.

"I just got back from town. You killed Price at that bluff and you shot Lentz Diamond in the leg. He'll be crippled for life. Doc had to take the leg off above the knee. So Diamond's put out a five-hundred-dollar reward for you, dead or alive. And he's burned your livery stable and your house."

Mrs. Egan continued warming the meal for Mike. Beyond glancing once at her husband, she paid no attention to the gun. Warmer now, Mike stepped away from the stove. Egan said nervously, "Easy now. Don't do anything stupid or I'll put a hole in you."

"How are you going to get me to town?"

Egan looked momentarily puzzled. He was a short and stocky man with a broad face and a head half bald. He had blue eyes, a rather thick-lipped mouth, and a nose that had been broken and flattened in countless fights. He said, "Turn around. Put your hands up in the air."

Mike knew what Egan was going to do. He was going to hit him with the rifle and knock him out.

And suddenly Mike had had enough. Fury blazed in his mind. The coffee cup was still half full, and, almost without thinking about it, he flung it straight into Egan's face. He lunged forward as he did, and Egan brought the gun up, as if to fire it.

Mrs. Egan screamed, "No! You might hit me!" and Egan let the hammer down without firing. Mike closed with him and Egan brought the rifle up and slammed it forward, half blinded, but aiming either at Mike's throat or face.

The rifle caught him in the throat. It almost collapsed his windpipe despite the collar of his heavy sheepskin coat. But he got his own hands on it and for a moment the two wrestled for possession of it, with Mike realizing that Egan was as strong as a bull, fully a match for him even if he had been unwounded, rested, and strong.

Egan yanked hard on the rifle and Mike suddenly let go. Egan staggered back across the kitchen, smashed into the table and chairs, and collapsed to the floor in the wreckage of a smashed chair and an overturned table. Mike plunged after him. Egan still had the rifle, and now, with his vision clear again, he tried to bring it to bear.

Mike kicked at the rifle, missed it, but connected instead with the side of Egan's head. Stunned, Egan sprawled backward and Mike followed, stopping now to seize the gun while he had the chance.

Bent over this way, he didn't hear Mrs. Egan coming at him from behind. The hot skillet came down squarely on the top of his head. Hot grease showered him, most of it harmlessly splattering his hat and the collar and shoulders of his coat.

Cushioned by his hat, the skillet stunned but did not knock him out. He fell to one side, giving himself added impetus by pushing off with his hands. He knew that that damned skillet would hit him again if he didn't get out of its way, and the second blow might put him out.

The chicken she had been warming in the skillet lay scattered on the floor amid the table's wreckage and the sprawled body of Lester Egan. The rifle was now out of

Mike Logan's reach. He jammed a hand into the pocket of his coat, felt the revolver grips, and yanked. The hammer caught on his coat and he could see Egan swinging the rifle around. This time Egan wouldn't threaten with it; he'd shoot.

Mike gave the revolver another frantic yank and this time it cleared. He thumbed back the hammer and bawled, "Hold it, Les, or I'll blow a hole in you!"

The rifle was not yet directly bearing on him. Egan froze, stared a moment, and then lowered the rifle to the floor. Mrs. Egan remained where she was, the skillet in her hand. Mike said, "Take it back to the stove."

Meekly she obeyed. Mike said, "Pick up the chicken and wipe it off. I still need something to eat."

She came back with a plate and began gathering up the chicken. Mike got to his feet, walked to Egan, and held out his left hand for the rifle. Egan gave it to him. Mike ejected the shells, threw the rifle into a corner, and then, one by one, picked up the shells.

Egan righted the table and gathered up the pieces of the smashed chair. Mike crossed to the table, put his back to the wall, and sat down. He laid his revolver on the table beside his plate. He looked at Mrs. Egan. "Have you got any bread and milk?"

Silently she brought him some. Mike said, "The two of you go on over to the other side of the room and sit down until I'm through."

They obeyed sullenly and Mike began to eat. He asked, "Know why I killed Reese?"

Both of them dumbly shook their heads.

Mike said, "I caught him trying to rip Martha Lansing's

clothes off right in front of her two little kids. She was fighting but she was no match for Reese."

Mrs. Egan said, "Mr. Diamond didn't tell Les that."

Mike said, "I chased him out into the storm. He shot me in the shoulder before I ever fired at him. I don't suppose Diamond told Les that either."

Both of them shook their heads. Mike said, "Diamond said he'd hunt me down like a wolf. The sheriff said he couldn't do a thing about Diamond's threats but he'd arrest him after I'd been killed. That didn't seem good enough for me."

Mrs. Egan looked contrite even if her husband did not. She said, "We didn't know. And five hundred dollars . . ."

Mike said, "All right." He finished the last piece of chicken and drained what was left of the milk. "I'll be going." He was completely warm now, sweating even from the fight, but his shoulder ached terribly and he could feel the warm wetness of blood on the bandages.

He got up and went toward the kitchen door. He looked at Egan. "Don't follow me. And don't go to Diamond. If you do, I'll tell him you helped me of your own free will."

He doubted if Diamond would believe that, but the threat might give Egan second thoughts. Besides, Mrs. Egan seemed genuinely sorry for what had happened here.

He went out, closing the door behind him. He still had the revolver in his hand and he waited several moments outside the door to see what Egan was going to do.

He heard the murmur of voices inside, but no one came out the door, and at last, satisfied that Egan would take no chances until he was sure Mike had gone, he headed for the barn.

His horses had finished the hay. Mike put the revolver back into his coat pocket, replaced the bit in his horse's mouth, put on his gloves, and mounted. He rode out, leading the packhorse.

He didn't hesitate about where he wanted to go. Diamond had burned his house and barn. That was a debt that had to be repaid.

CHAPTER ELEVEN

The stop at Egan's had not only warmed Mike. He had eaten well. He felt stronger than he had since he had been shot. The warmth of blood beneath the shoulder bandages told him the fight had reopened his wound, but he figured the wound would clot and close again before too much blood had been lost.

Now that he was away from Egan and from the tension of having to be on guard against the man, he thought about Jasper Diamond vengefully burning his livery stable and his house. That meant everything he had in the world was gone. His means of livelihood had been destroyed, and, not satisfied with that, Diamond had left him with no place to go. So far he hadn't been able to make good his boast that he'd hunt Mike down like a wolf, so he had destroyed everything Mike possessed.

Fortunately, the wind had begun to die when the sun set, and the air right now was almost calm. The ground blizzard was over with. The sky was clear, studded with blinking stars.

But with the passing of the clouds and wind, bitter, savage cold had settled upon the land. Mike had no way of knowing, of course, exactly how cold it was. From his experience and from the way his nostrils felt when he breathed, he guessed it was between fifteen and twenty below. Ice formed on his coat collar where he breathed on it. And despite the warmth that had returned to his body at Egan's, he now began to chill again.

First his shoulder began to ache from cold. Then his hands began to stiffen and hurt. Lastly, his legs and feet turned numb. But it wasn't far to Diamond's place and he could probably get warm there. If nobody was present, he'd build a fire that would keep him warm all night. A big fire. The kind Diamond had built in town.

It was late when he brought Diamond's place in sight. It was an impressive-looking place. Tall poplars lined the lane leading down to it. Around the buildings, particularly the house, there were cottonwoods, their leaves, even in darkness, even with their light covering of snow, a flaming yellow.

The house itself was built in the style of the time. It was three stories high, and the windows on the third story were gabled, with white-painted shutters that could be closed.

A wide, covered veranda circled the house on three sides. In the rear was a huge, screened-in porch. A water tank stood in the back yard beside a windmill, high enough to put water pressure into all three floors of the house.

Not a light showed anywhere, but Mike circled the place anyhow and came upon it from the rear. There was an old soddy down by the creek, from which the door had long since disappeared. Mike took his horses there and led them inside. They seemed content, in no hurry to leave the shelter of the place, which would warm their bodies to a temperature twenty or so degrees above that outside.

Mike walked to a nearby haystack. A fork was sticking into it and it wasn't over ten feet high, having been used for feeding horses and milk cows kept near the house. A ladder leaned against it. He climbed up and, trying to ignore the pain in his shoulder, threw down a generous amount of hay. Climbing down again, he carried the hay to the soddy and threw it in for his two horses to eat. He didn't loosen either cinch, but he did take the bit out of his saddle horse's mouth.

Turning, he stared at the buildings again. It was late and whoever might be present had undoubtedly gone to bed. There had to be a choreman and a cook. There could be several others and Mike had no desire to be responsible for any more deaths, particularly of men who had done him no harm.

Furthermore, he needed rest. He glanced back at the soddy. The door faced toward the creek, away from the house. Even if Diamond returned, which wasn't likely this late at night, it was doubtful that they would expect his presence here.

It was his chance to get some sleep, sleep that might later mean the difference between survival and death.

He climbed on the haystack again and forked down another good-sized pile of hay. He carried it, a forkful at a time, to the soddy and threw it inside. He returned the fork to the haystack, then walked back to the soddy. He went just inside the door and lay down, burrowing down into the hay for warmth. If anybody did, by chance, come to the soddy door, they wouldn't see him right away. They'd see hay and two horses eating it, but they would not see him. That might give him the slight edge he'd need.

He lay there drowsily, trying not to think about his house and livery barn. But he couldn't help himself. House and livery barn represented the work of his lifetime. He still owned a few horses, maybe fifteen or twenty in all, which he rented out. But all the buggies, buckboards, and wagons that had been inside the livery stable were gone. They had burned with it.

He'd have to start over from scratch—if he was alive to do anything when this was over with. And what about Martha? She'd said she would marry him, and she probably still would, but how would he support her with everything he owned burned up?

That doubt was disquieting for only a moment or two. He'd supported himself pretty well since he was fifteen years old. He had a few horses to give himself a new start. And Martha had a house. They'd make it. But not as long as Diamond was hunting him. Mike reluctantly faced the fact that he would have no peace as long as Jasper Diamond lived.

His thoughts slowed and finally stopped. His last memory was of Martha Lansing, tears in her eyes, tears for him. And then he slept.

Gray dawn awakened him. He was reasonably warm but the horses were now eating the hay that covered him, having finished the hay he had given them. He opened his eyes, lying very still, trying to decide what had awakened him.

He heard it then, again. It was the slamming of the outhouse door. He got up, brushing hay from his clothes, and poked his head around the corner of the soddy so that he could see the house.

The cook, clad only in sheepskin coat, boots, and his long underwear, was heading for the kitchen door. Mike returned to the soddy door, went in, and put the bit into his saddle horse's mouth. Leaving both horses there, he again went to the corner of the soddy. The cook had disappeared into the house. A thin plume of smoke rose from the chimney.

Mike spent several minutes studying the frosty, wind-scoured yard. He saw no tracks or other signs of life. No smoke rose from the bunkhouse chimney, so he assumed that whatever crewmen were here had not yet gotten out of bed.

Walking slowly, head burrowed into his coat collar, hat pulled low over his eyes. Mike walked at a normal pace toward the barn. If he *was* seen it would probably be assumed that he was one of the crew. He kept a sharp eye on the back door of the house and on the bunkhouse door. Nobody appeared.

He reached the barn door and went inside. It was only open a foot and a half and he had to turn sideways to get inside.

There were horses in the barn, maybe ten or twelve of them, warm and comfortable in stalls, with hay in the manger that ran the length of the stalls.

Leaving the door no farther open than he had found it,

Mike went to each stall and unbuckled the halter that secured each horse. They left their stalls and milled near the door, waiting to be let out.

Mike climbed the ladder to the loft. He guessed there must be more than twenty tons of hay stored here. He fumbled in his pocket for a match, found it, and struck it against the ladder. He waited until it flared, then placed it carefully beneath the nearest hay.

Flame ran upward across the stored hay like water pouring over a waterfall but reversed. Mike waited until it reached the roof, until he was sure it could not be put out. Then he descended the ladder.

The horses, smelling smoke, were milling around excitedly, some of them snorting nervously. Mike pushed his way through them and opened wide the big barn doors. The horses thundered out.

Mike knew the noise of their leaving would awaken whoever was still asleep, would bring outside whoever was awake but inside the kitchen or bunkhouse. He sprinted for the soddy, rounded the corner, and disappeared. He led his saddle horse and packhorse outside.

He mounted, dug heels into his horse's sides. The packhorse nearly pulled the halter rope out of his hands, being slow to start, but Mike managed to hang on.

Glancing back, he saw smoke billowing from both open doors of the enormous barn. He saw several men running from the bunkhouse, clad only in long underwear and boots. None of them carried guns. Nor did the cook, who came running from the back door of the house.

Seeing Mike, one of the crewmen ran back into the

bunkhouse and came running out again with a gun. He fired twice at Mike, but by then Mike was too far away.

Others of the crew, two of them, ran into the barn and dragged out one buggy. After that, salvaging anything was impossible. The fire burned through the roof and flames shot twenty feet into the air. Mike disappeared over the nearest rise. After that, whenever he looked back he could see the towering column of smoke. He could still see it when it was several miles away.

He felt rested and refreshed. Most of all, he felt a vast satisfaction that he had struck a return blow at Jasper Diamond. Maybe it wasn't the equal of what Diamond had done to him, but it was a blow that Jasper Diamond would feel and one that would infuriate him monumentally.

It was all-out war. Diamond wouldn't rest until Mike Logan was dead. And Mike Logan didn't dare rest until Jasper Diamond was dead.

For a while Mike rode aimlessly. He didn't know where to go. He was determined not to let Jasper Diamond drive him out of the country and he was aware of the fact that he was leaving a trail that a child could follow.

But the sun shone warmly down, and he was more comfortable than he had been since he had first been driven out into the blowing snow.

Sun, shining on his back, thoroughly warmed his wounded shoulder and decreased the ache in it. He was hungry, but decided against trying to stop to fix himself a hot meal. He didn't know how many of Diamond's crewmen had been at the ranch and he didn't know but what those who had been would pursue him as soon as they gave up on trying to save the barn.

In late October, the sun could still get pretty hot. By eight, the land was steaming in the places where the wind had scoured off the snow. By nine, water was running in the gulches. By ten, the snow was gone except for those places where the wind had drifted it several feet deep.

Now, Mike realized, he could once more hide his trail. All that was necessary was for him to ride into one of the gulches that had not drifted full of snow and was running with several inches of water, and follow it to a fork where another such gulch ran into it. He'd force those pursuing him to split up, some following one gulch, the others following the other branch. When the opportunity came, which he knew it would, he'd force them to split again. Eventually the chance would come to lose them all. If he left a print or two he'd just have to hope that the sun would thaw the snow and obliterate it.

He rode down into the first small gulch he reached, careful to ride in as if he intended to ride upstream. But as soon as all four of his horse's hooves were in the water, he reversed direction and rode downstream with the water flow.

This way, he continued for half a mile. Then he reached a fork, where another, smaller gulch flowed into the first. He turned, rode up the smaller gulch, letting just one hoofprint show at one side of the water flow.

Grinning faintly, he backed the horse to the original gulch and continued down it for another half mile.

The water was now getting pretty deep. A foot or so.

He found another gulch and this time took the smaller
one, careful to stay in the water and let no hoofprints
show.

This gulch divided about a mile farther on, but by now
the sun was almost directly overhead and both forks had
six inches of water flowing in them.

Mike selected the smaller of the two because it led toward a rocky knoll that faced south and ought to be
nearly dry.

He reached it, surprised to discover a shallow ravine
leading up toward the top of the rocky knoll. Because of
the shade it had received, this shallow ravine was still
covered with two or three inches of melting snow.

On impulse, Mike turned his horses and took the ravine, careful to stay in the snow, careful to hold his horses
to a slow walk so that their hooves would make no inden-
tations in the ground beneath the snow.

Glancing behind, he could see no pursuers. Grinning
faintly to himself, he continued to the top of the ridge,
where he paused to scan the horizon behind.

He still saw no one behind. He let his glance shift to
the snow-filled ravine where his tracks plainly showed.

The whole land had begun to steam for as far as the
eye could see. Even as he watched, the sun shone full into
the shallow ravine and began to melt the snow where his
horses' hooves had made their marks in it.

An hour, he thought. If he had an hour, all the snow in
that shallow ravine would be gone, along with the tracks
his horses had made in it. And he could feel safe again.

He wanted to go to Rafael Castillo's place. He knew he
could get his wound dressed there, knew he could get a

hot meal and maybe, if he needed it, a change of horses whose tracks Diamond's men would not recognize.

And he could do it now without leading Diamond's men to the place. He could do it without placing Rafael in jeopardy.

CHAPTER TWELVE

Now that the storm was over and the sun out, landmarks were visible for miles. Mike was able to set a direct course from where he now was to Rafael Castillo's place. He reached it about mid-afternoon, not hurrying his horses but letting them travel at a walk. He didn't know how much longer he was going to have to work them and he didn't want to change horses unless it was absolutely necessary. He knew these two and knew exactly what to expect from them.

Castillo's place lay back where the foothills began and was nestled in a shallow draw where a small spring-fed stream ran all year 'round. Rafael had dammed it above the house, fenced off the dam, and then run a pipe down from the dam to a large tank just behind the house.

Mike circled around behind Castillo's house, then watched it from there for several minutes before he rode in. The road leading from Castillo's to town was empty. There were no fresh tracks in it and no horses were in the yard between Castillo's house and the barn.

As Mike rode down the slope, he could hear the clang of a hammer in the barn, so he went that way. Castillo was working at a forge, flattening a piece of strap iron to repair a wagon that stood nearby. He glanced up when he heard Mike.

Immediately he glanced beyond Mike, and from the way his face looked, Mike knew he had heard about Reese Diamond's death. Mike asked, "How much of it do you know?"

"One of Diamond's crewmen quit. That new one, Sturges. Got in a fight with Diamond and walked off. He came by here on his way north. He told me all of it. About Reese. About you crippling Lentz and killing one of his crew. Sturges said Diamond had your barn burned and your house. The sheriff's got Hank Diamond in jail, charged with arson. Hank bought a can of coal oil at the store just before your house burned down."

Mike nodded. He was keeping track of the odds against him. Sturges leaving and Hank being jailed left Diamond with his two remaining sons, Hugo and Rudy, and three crewmen, not counting the cook and the choreman, neither of whom would be any good on a chase. Six against one. Still long odds.

Mike said, "I spent the night at Diamond's place. Fed and rested my horses and burned his barn after I heard he'd burned my stable and my house."

Castillo whistled. "I'd hate to be around when he finds that out!"

Mike said, "Reese shot me in the shoulder before I killed him. Martha tied it up, but it's been bleeding and it needs rebandaging. Do you think your wife . . . ?"

"Sure. Come on." Castillo laid down his blacksmith's hammer on the anvil, wiped his hands on his blacksmith's apron, and led the way toward the house. Mike left his horses standing. They'd eaten and rested well enough last night and he wanted them ready in case Diamond should show up. There weren't too many places in this area where Mike could get help, and this was one of them.

Rosita, Castillo's sixteen-year-old daughter, was in the kitchen with her mother, an ample, pleasant-faced Mexican woman. Rosita kept her glance on Mike, but every time he glanced at her, she blushed and glanced away in confusion. Mike knew she had a girlish crush on him and he was flattered. He smiled at her once as Castillo explained to his wife what needed to be done.

Mike took off his coat as carefully as he could, his face twisting with the pain of the shoulder wound. His shirt and underwear were stuck to the bandages with blood. Mrs. Castillo had him sit down in a chair in the middle of the room while she poured a basin full of warm water from the stove.

She pulled his shirt carefully away in the places it was stuck, and carefully eased it off. She did the same with the upper part of his underwear, which was not stuck as badly due to the fact that the wound had bled considerably recently. Then she began unwinding the bandages.

Mike gripped the sides of the chair and pressed himself against its back. Waves of weakness passed over him. He suddenly realized how helpless he was just now, and how much trust he was placing in this family. If they had heard about the killing of Reese, the crippling of Lentz, and the killing of Diamond's crewman, as well as the burning of his stable and house, it was likely they also had heard about the five-hundred-dollar reward. And that was a lot of money to a family trying to scratch a living out of these barren hills.

Mrs. Castillo carefully removed the last of the bandages Martha had put on. Still holding on desperately, Mike glanced aside at the wound. The skin all around it was red and swollen but he didn't know if that was normal or if it meant he was developing blood poisoning. He was vastly relieved when Mrs. Castillo said, "It looks all right. Rosita, get me that old sheet in the bureau drawer. Rafael, get some of that precious whiskey of yours."

Rosita, whose face now was deathly white, left the room. Rafael got a bottle of whiskey out of a cupboard and brought it to his wife. She pulled the cork and handed it to Mike. "You look like you could use a little of this before I put it on the wound."

He knew what the whiskey was going to feel like when it hit the wound. He put the bottle to his mouth and drank as much as he could. Then he gave the bottle back.

Rosita returned with the sheet. Mrs. Castillo tore strips from it, careful that they touched nothing but the spotless tabletop. She made two compresses and soaked each with whiskey. Then, placing one each on the entry and exit wounds, she began to wind the bandage around to hold them in place, loosely so that when the wound swelled, which it would, they would not then be too tight.

Finished, she ripped the end about two feet down and tied the two ends. She helped Mike, whose face was now a ghastly shade of grayish green, to get his underwear back over it, and helped him on with his shirt. By the time it was buttoned, he was sweating profusely. Castillo asked, "You want something to eat?"

"I couldn't eat now. And I've got food on my saddle." He looked at Mrs. Castillo. "You think that shoulder wound is all right?"

She nodded. "The red is natural. It's not infection."

"I can't thank you enough."

"*De nada.*"

Mike headed for the door. Just outside, he heard Mrs. Castillo say something to her husband that he didn't understand. He heard Castillo reply, but again he couldn't understand. He headed for his horses. He knew he ought to rest here for a while but something he couldn't name had suddenly made him feel uneasy here.

There seemed no logical reason for uneasiness. Certainly they had helped him. They had done everything he had asked. He reached his horses, picked up the halter rope of his packhorse, and climbed awkwardly to his saddle because of the pain in his shoulder.

He turned to ride past the house and back the way he had come in.

Castillo stepped out of the doorway, a rifle in his hands. He jacked a cartridge into the chamber and raised the gun. "Don't go, Mike. I'm turning you in for the reward."

Mike stared at him unbelievingly.

Mike saw Rosita's face a couple of feet behind her father. He said, "You know he'll kill me, don't you? He won't turn me over to the law."

Castillo looked ashamed. He started to lower the gun, but stopped when his wife's voice said sharply, "Rafael! Do you know what five hundred dollars will mean to us?"

Mike had no intention of letting himself be taken. But he was hampered by his packhorse, and he knew that if he tried to make a run for it he'd get shot. Even if the bullet didn't kill him, there'd be no way he could keep going with two bullet wounds.

Suddenly, behind her father, Rosita moved. She threw her body against her father's back and sent him staggering out the door. He stumbled on the single step and sprawled on the ground. The gun discharged.

Mike wasted no time. He dug spurs into his horse. The packhorse's lead rope nearly dragged his good arm out of its socket but he held on. Then both horses were running hard up the shallow gulch behind the house.

Mike kept waiting for the sound of a second shot but it never came. At the top of the hill he looked back. Castillo, his wife, and Rosita stood together watching him. Mike rode over the crest and they were lost to sight.

He was disappointed in Rafael and his wife. He'd thought they were his friends and that he could count on them.

But could he blame them? Five hundred dollars was probably more money than they'd ever seen. They knew, furthermore, that if Diamond ever found out they had helped him, reprisal might be swift and devastating. Diamond had burned Mike's stable and his house. He might burn out anybody who gave him help. And Rosita. He smiled faintly to himself. Rosita had helped him when it counted and he would always be grateful to her for that.

Sheriff Bondy saddled up as soon as the fires were under control and headed for the Diamond Ranch. By recklessly spurring his horse, he was able to overtake Diamond, his remaining sons, and his crew before they were much more than two miles out of town. They heard him and stopped. Bondy jerked a cartridge into his rifle and rode straight to Diamond, sitting huge and bulky in his saddle in the driving wind. Bondy said, "I want Hank. For arson. He bought a can of coal oil less than ten minutes before Mike Logan's house was burned."

Diamond said harshly, "You go straight to hell!"

Bondy was angry by now himself. Maybe he couldn't do anything about the way they were hounding Mike. Maybe he couldn't prove that they had fired his livery barn. But he could prove Hank had bought a can of coal oil just before the fire broke out at Mike Logan's house. And he was willing to bet he'd find the can right there beside the house, or inside, probably still recognizable enough. He said, evenly, without raising his voice, "Mr. Diamond, you're the one headed straight for hell unless you give me Hank. This rifle is loaded and cocked and pointed straight at your gut."

For a moment nobody said anything. Finally Diamond said, "Go with him, Hank. I'll get you out in a day or two."

Bondy said, "Head back for town, Hank. But first give the man nearest you your gun."

Out of the corner of his eye he watched the transfer without taking his full glance off Diamond's bulky shape. When the gun had been handed over, Bondy said, "Head for town, Hank. Keep your horse at a walk."

Hank's horse moved out. Bondy backed his horse and Diamond's remaining sons and crewmen got out of the way. When he was well clear, Bondy called, "All right. Go on home. And my advice would be to leave Mike Logan to the law."

Nobody said anything. Diamond turned and rode away, his sons and crewmen following. Bondy turned his horse and quickly caught up with Hank. He reached out and took the reins of Hank's horse. Hank had turned his rifle over to another of the men but Bondy didn't know whether or not he had a revolver beneath his coat. In any event, it wasn't likely he'd be able to get it out right now. His hands must be at least as numb as Bondy's were, and his coat was equally bulky.

He reached town and dismounted in front of the jail. Hank went in and Bondy followed him, glad now that he had left one lamp turned low. He said, "Take your coat off."

Hank complied. There was a revolver belted around his waist. Bondy said, "Let it drop and step away from it."

Again Hank complied. Bondy marched him back to a cell and locked him in. There was no resentment on Hank Diamond's face. Instead, there was something that looked like relief.

Bondy realized that Hank was glad to be out of it. He thought that maybe some of the others might feel the same. He shrugged fatalistically. Even if they did, there was still Jasper Diamond. He would never give up until Mike Logan was dead. And if his men talked of deserting him, he'd pay them enough to persuade them to stay on.

Mike's only chance lay in getting clear out of the country and staying gone. That was the only way he was going to stay alive.

CHAPTER THIRTEEN

———◆———

Jasper Diamond rode steadily toward home, holding his horse to a walk. The monumental anger he had felt upon discovering that Reese was dead, and later that Lentz was crippled, had now increased, if such was possible. The sheriff had taken Hank and jailed him on a charge of arson for doing only what his father had told him to.

Suddenly he hauled his horse to a halt. His two other sons and Harrison also stopped. Diamond said, "We're going back."

Nobody argued with him. All seemed glad enough to be returning to town. He headed his horse back along the road toward town. The livery stable was gone, so he didn't know where he'd put the horses, but there were a few good-sized private stables in Chimney Rock. One belonged to Seward, who ran the general store. Seward wouldn't object to letting them stable their horses there.

In his mind he kept fretting about Hank in jail. If they ever found that coal-oil can, they might send Hank to prison for several years. He'd bought the coal oil at Seward's Store minutes before Mike's house had broken into flame. He had a reason for wanting to hurt Mike, since

Mike had killed one of his brothers and crippled a second. All that might save him was if his father, brothers, and members of the crew recovered the coal-oil can and got rid of it. Without that evidence, Hank would have a chance.

As he rode, Diamond tried to remember what he'd done with the coal-oil can. He supposed he had just thrown it aside inside the house after pouring its contents over the bed and the rest of the furniture. Unless the fire had been hot enough to melt it down, which he doubted, it probably was still there, in the cooling embers of the house. Somehow they had to get hold of it before the sheriff did.

It was very late when they rode into town. Diamond looked first at the sheriff's office to see if there was a light inside. There was not. He dismounted and handed the reins of his horse to Harrison. To Rudy he said, "Let Harrison take your horse. He and Hugo can put 'em in Seward's stable for tonight. You and me are going to see if we can get that coal-oil can."

Rudy got down and the other two disappeared into the stormy night with the horses.

There was still a lot of heat coming from the embers of Mike Logan's house. But there was a shed and stable large enough for one horse out in back of it, which hadn't burned. Diamond went straight to the shed. He found a shovel inside and a pitchfork inside the stable. He handed the shovel to his son and said, "Come on."

The snow for twenty-five feet on all sides of Mike's house had melted, and was now a sea of mud, trampled by all the people who had come to watch the blaze. Diamond headed for the front of the house. Embers still glowed in the wind, and ashes still lifted and swirled away. But most of the fire had been killed by water drawn from the well and thrown on it by the townspeople.

Diamond knew he didn't dare step over the foundations and into the perimeter of what had formerly been the walls. So he got as close as he could, peering, sometimes stirring the ashes with the pitchfork he held in his hands.

Numerous metal objects clanged upon the tines. But finally he touched something that sounded hollow. Softly he called, "Rudy, I think it's here."

He probed some more, reaching as far as he could, getting the pitchfork on top of the object and each time rolling it a little bit closer to him. At last he hooked a pitchfork tine in the handle of the can and lifted it clear. He put it down and handed the pitchfork to Rudy. "Put 'em back in the shed. Then come back here. By that time the damn thing ought to be cool."

He waited until Rudy returned. Gingerly he touched the wire handle of the can and discovered that it was cool. Rudy asked, "What are you goin' to do with it?"

Diamond frowned. Finally he said, "Take it down to the creek. Throw it in. By the time the run-off from this snow is over with, it'll be twenty miles downstream."

Rudy departed with the can. Softly Diamond called after him, "Then come to the hotel. We'll spend the night in town."

He walked back toward the center of town. His other son, Hugo, and Harrison were waiting uncertainly in front of the hotel. Diamond said, "Come on. We'll stay in town tonight. Tomorrow at dawn we'll get after Logan again."

He went into the hotel, woke the clerk, and got rooms for himself, his sons, and Harrison. They tramped upstairs, waited while the clerk buit a fire in each of the rooms, then wearily undressed, blew out the lamps, and went to bed.

Diamond did not immediately go to sleep. He had probably saved Hank by getting rid of the coal-oil can. But Lentz was still crippled and Reese was dead. And Mike Logan still was free.

Well, he had to go someplace. He'd go to Egan's, or to Castillo's, because they were closest. Or else he'd get out of the country for good.

Diamond didn't think that likely. For one thing, Logan was courting the Lansing woman. For another, he wasn't going to take kindly to having his house and livery stable burned. No, he'd stay. And Diamond would find him and string him up.

But his crew was shrinking. Reese was gone and Lentz was out of it. So was Hank. Sturges had quit after the burning of Logan's livery stable and house, saying there were plenty of jobs that didn't require a man to do this kind of thing.

Even so, with himself he still had four—plenty to run Mike Logan down once the storm had stopped. And it looked as if tomorrow the storm was going to stop. Today he'd caught several glimpses of clear blue sky through the blowing snow. By morning, the ground blizzard would probably be over with and the sun would shine. The snow would melt but there'd still be enough of it and enough mud that Mike couldn't help but leave a trail.

He went to sleep. As usual, he awoke half an hour before dawn, and sat up on the side of the bed immediately. The fire had burned itself out, and the room was cold as ice. He dressed, shivering, then went out into the hall and roused his sons and Harrison by yelling at them. They were out of the hotel, mounted, and headed toward home by the time the sun came up.

Diamond saw the smoke in the sky while he was still half a mile from home. He kicked his horse into a lope immediately, and as he came over the last, low rise he saw that the barn was gone. The place where it formerly stood was now only a pile of blackened timbers and some glowing, smoldering coals.

Mike Logan, damn his soul to hell, had retaliated in kind. For the burning of his livery stable and his house, he had burned Jasper Diamond's barn. And he had probably run all the horses out, which meant they'd have to be rounded up again before he and his men could have fresh mounts.

Diamond spurred his horse and came into the yard at a run. The Chinese cook, Wong, and the choreman, Gebhardt, were still out in the yard, all the buckets they could find around them. Tubbs and Gargan were with them. The four had been dousing other buildings with water so that they couldn't catch from the barn. They all looked so cold and wet and miserable that Diamond said, "Go on inside. Get warm and put on some food. We're all hungry. We'll be in as soon as we put these horses away someplace."

The cook, the choreman, and the two crewmen went into the house. Diamond led the way to the corral. It was empty, which meant there wasn't a fresh horse on the place. To Harrison, Diamond said, "Get yourself warm and get something to eat and then take the trail of those damned horses. We'll all need fresh mounts as soon as we've finished eating."

They all dismounted and turned their worn-out horses into the corral. All unsaddled, except for Harrison, who left his saddle on. They trooped into the house.

Jasper Diamond's fury was like a hot fire burning in his gut. His skin felt hot all over his body, but particularly on his face. His hands trembled with it. He could have fought and killed Logan with his bare hands and reveled during every instant of it.

Fists clenched, he stamped into the kitchen, crossed to the stove, and spread his hands by it. He turned his great, shaggy head and glared at Wong, Gebhardt, Tubbs, and Gargan. "Where the hell were you when he burned the barn?"

Anger flared in the old choreman's eyes and in those of Tubbs and Gargan but the Chinese cook only cowered and looked scared. Gebhardt, the choreman, was sixty-five. He had worked for Diamond more than fifteen years and was unable to ride now only because of a fall taken while he was on Diamond's payroll. He tried to keep his anger from showing without success. "Where would you expect us to be out in a storm like this? Wong was in the kitchen and the rest of us were in bed. First thing we knew about the barn was the light of the fire coming in the window. We went out and we've been working like hell ever since to make sure nothing else caught from it."

Diamond grunted. He didn't apologize. The men shed hats and coats and sat down at the table. Diamond got a bottle of whiskey for them. Wong worked steadily at the stove and soon the kitchen was filled with the savory aroma of cooking meat.

Wong finally served the food and the men ate wolfishly. Harrison finished first and went out to trail the horses. Diamond said, "In case you're all resenting this ertra work, there's a hundred dollars apiece in it for you as soon as Logan's caught or killed. The man that kills him gets the five-hundred-dollar reward."

That picked them up. When Harrison brought the horse herd galloping in, they all went out to catch fresh mounts and saddle them.

Diamond was trying to decide what would be the best way to start. The sun was bright and the sky was clear. He would try trailing Mike Logan but there was a good chance that it would take a long time to unravel what trail he had made.

But there was another way. They could go to Martha Lansing's place, put out the word that they were there, and eventually Mike Logan would come to them. He'd take the bait like a hungry wolf, particularly if he thought there was a chance Diamond or his crewmen were mistreating her. Then Diamond could spring the trap.

Diamond went outside. As the door slammed behind him, he told Gebhardt, "You got a job here because you got hurt working for me. But if anything else gets burned, you're through. You understand?"

Gebhardt nodded sullenly, his eyes on the ground. Diamond mounted the horse Hugo brought him and rode away. Gebhardt raised his eyes, which he had kept lowered to conceal the resentment in them. It wasn't his fault the barn had been burned. It was Jasper Diamond's. Martha Lansing was a good woman trying her best to raise two little kids. Reese had been trying to force her and he'd gotten exactly what was coming to him. But Gebhardt also knew he needed this job with Diamond and that speaking out would serve no useful purpose anyway. He found himself a place in the sun from which he could see in all directions and sat down, a rifle across his knees. He wouldn't shoot to kill if Mike Logan showed up. But he'd scare the man away.

Jasper Diamond led away toward Martha Lansing's place. The snow began to melt, the ground turned muddy, and water began to run in the draws.

They reached Martha Lansing's lane. Diamond stared down at it. There wasn't a fresh print in it. Suspiciously he stared at the house.

To his men he said, "Spread out. Come at it from all directions. I'll wait here until all of you are set."

He watched them scatter, Tubbs, Harrison, and Rudy to the right, Hugo and Gargan to the left. They had to find gates in the barbed-wire fence, but within fifteen minutes all five were in place. Diamond gave them an arm signal and rode down the lane, knowing he was the most vulnerable of the six. If Mike Logan was here . . .

But no shots came from the house. He reached the door at about the same time the others did. The door opened, and Martha Lansing stood there, an old muzzle-loading rifle in her hands. Diamond said, "Put that down. We're not going to hurt you, but if you shoot that thing we'll burn everything you've got."

She hesitated a moment, then lowered the muzzle of the gun, which wasn't loaded anyway. She knew she had no chance against six armed and determined men. Diamond dismounted and pushed rudely past her into the house. Hugo and Rudy followed. Diamond looked around to make sure Logan wasn't here, then stuck his head out the door. "Harrison, you go to town and pass the word that we're here. Tell whoever you see that unless Mike Logan gives himself up, we're going to burn this place to the ground."

He looked at another of the men, Russ Gargan. "You make the rounds of the ranches with the same word. Go to Egan's and Castillo's and any others within half a day's ride from here."

The two men rode away. The remaining crewman, Tubbs, put the horses into the corral, only loosening the cinches and taking the bits out of the horses' mouths. He got a generous amount of Martha's precious hay from the loft of the shed where the cows were kept and threw it into the corral. Then he went back to the house.

Diamond stationed him at one of the front windows. He himself stood at the one in the bedroom where Martha and her two children slept.

Martha sat down at the table near the kitchen stove, one child on each side of her, an arm around each of them.

She had no idea where Mike Logan was, but she was pretty sure he hadn't left the country. Sooner or later he'd get the word that Diamond's men were passing out and then he'd come here.

Silently she began to pray that he wouldn't come, that he'd realize that her house, her possessions, weren't worth his life.

Diamond had made no threats to hurt her or the children. She tried to think of something she could do. But there wasn't anything. Not now. All she could do was wait.

CHAPTER FOURTEEN

———◆———

Bondy was in his office when Harrison rode into town. Immediately curious, he stepped outside into the bright morning sunlight. Snow lay drifted deeply on the lee sides of all the buildings. Down where the livery stable had been was only a blackened spot from which a few wisps of smoke still arose. Harrison tried to avoid looking at the sheriff, but he had no choice when Bondy yelled, "Harrison! Come over here!"

Harrison hedged. "Any law that says a man can't ride into town?"

"Don't play games with me. I can throw you in with Hank."

"On what charge?"

"Who needs a charge? Better answer my question."

"Mr. Diamond sent me."

"To do what?"

"To pass the word that he was out at Martha Lansing's. That he was going to burn her out unless Logan gave himself up. Logan burned his barn last night."

Bondy looked at him disgustedly. "So now Diamond is

making war on women and little kids. I thought he was
more man than that."

Harrison asked sullenly, "Can I go?"

"Sure. Go on. I don't even want to look at you."

The livery stable had been burned but there were a lot
of horses hanging around the open corral out back, some
inside, some out, because they didn't know where else to
go. Bondy locked the office door, then walked over to Sid
DeVoe's house.

Sid was in the kitchen eating breakfast. He invited
Bondy to join him and Bondy accepted gratefully. De-
Voe's wife served him and Bondy said, "Diamond is out at
Martha Lansing's place. He sent Harrison to town to pass
the word that unless Logan surrenders himself he's going
to burn her out."

"You going out there?"

"Uh-huh. That's why I came over here. I want you to
come along."

"Sure. Just as soon as we finish eating."

They finished quickly and both men got to their feet.
Bondy thanked Mrs. DeVoe. She said, "Be careful. It
sounds to me like Mr. Diamond is clear out of his head."

Bondy said, "Don't worry." But he was inclined to
agree with Mrs. DeVoe. Diamond had lost a son, killed by
Mike Logan. He had a second crippled for life, with his
leg amputated above the knee, also the result of Mike
Logan's shooting. His barn was gone, and it had been a
big one, filled with wagons and buggies and buckboards
and farming machinery as well as with a loft full of hay
put there no more than a month ago. And his son Hank
was in jail, charged with arson, a charge that would prob-

ably stick if he was able to salvage that coal-oil can out of the embers of Mike Logan's house later today when they had cooled enough.

He got a rope from one of the corral posts and caught himself a horse. He caught one for DeVoe. He found a couple of rope halters and gave DeVoe one, taking one himself. He said, "My saddle's down at the jail. You go on home and get yours and meet me there."

He leaped to the horse's back and rode him along the street to the jail. He tied him outside, then went in and got his saddle and bridle, brought them out, and put them on. He didn't have to wait long for Sid DeVoe. When Sid showed up, he mounted and the two rode out of town, heading north along the road to Martha Lansing's place.

Bondy wondered where Mike Logan was. He admitted to being secretly pleased that Mike had gotten back at Diamond for burning the livery stable and his house by burning Diamond's barn. He was also secretly pleased that, while he could probably produce enough evidence to convict Hank Diamond of arson, it was doubtful if there was a shred of evidence to prove Mike had fired Diamond's barn.

But his satisfaction didn't last very long. Diamond was at Martha Lansing's with his two remaining sons and with whatever was left of his crew. Sooner or later Mike would get the word that Diamond was passing out. When he did, he'd go to Martha's place and he'd probably get killed for his pains. Or captured and hanged, which would be worse. Bondy figured his only chance of stopping this madness was to arrest Jasper Diamond and hold him in jail until he calmed down.

There were still places where the two horses had to fight through two- or three-foot drifts but the sun was warm and the snow was melting fast. Already water was running in the dry gulches from the melt, and collecting in the ditches beside the road, which was muddy wherever it wasn't covered with snow.

They reached Martha Lansing's place and rode in. It never occurred to Bondy that Diamond would meet him with drawn guns, but that was exactly what Diamond did. His face unshaven, haggard, his eyes bloodshot and angry, he held a double-barreled shotgun on Bondy and DeVoe and said, "What the hell do you want?"

"You. You're under arrest."

"For what? Logan's the sonofabitch you ought to be looking for."

"You can't walk in and take possession of somebody's house and make them prisoners."

"What law says that?"

Bondy was at a loss. "Hell, I don't know. It's kidnapping, or breaking and entering, or something. That's up to the county attorney. All I know is that it's against the law."

Diamond's face was ugly. He turned his head and called, "Mrs. Lansing!"

She came to the door, a frightened child on each side of her. Her own face was terror-filled. Diamond asked, "Have we hurt you in any way?"

Dumbly she shook her head. But Bondy had seen enough. The terror in her face and in those of her children was enough. He said, "Put down the gun, Jasper. You're under arrest. And tell your men to go on home. I'll take care of enforcing the law."

Diamond's face flushed and his eyes got even uglier. Bondy hadn't drawn a gun. He hadn't thought it necessary. Not against someone like Diamond. Now Diamond said, "Get off your horses. Both of you."

The shotgun bores were as menacing as Diamond's eyes. And Bondy saw a quality in them that made him obey instantly. It was a kind of madness, as if Diamond was no longer in full control of himself.

Bondy dismounted, and Sid DeVoe followed suit. Bondy said, "Now unbutton your coats and shuck your guns." Bondy had a rifle in the saddle boot. Diamond stepped over to the horse, withdrew the gun, and threw it halfway across the yard.

Bondy hesitated just an instant. The shotgun swung back to cover him and he knew that if he didn't instantly obey, Diamond would shoot. He carefully unbuttoned his coat, unbuckled his gunbelt, and let it fall. He looked at DeVoe. "Better do it, Sid."

DeVoe unbuttoned his coat and got rid of his gun. Diamond looked at one of his men. "Get some rope."

The man disappeared into the shed where Martha Lansing kept her cows. He emerged a few moments later with a couple of lengths of rope. Diamond said, "Tie their hands. Behind their backs."

Bondy said, "Jasper, this is foolishness. All this is just going to make things go harder on you."

"Shut up. Do what you're told."

Bondy held his hands behind his back and let them be

tied. When both he and DeVoe were securely tied, Diamond said, "Put 'em on their horses. Not facin' forward. I want 'em facin' the horse's rump."

Bondy didn't bother to argue with the man any more. Diamond was clear out of his head and there was no telling what he might do if he was crossed. He allowed himself to be boosted onto his horse's back, facing the horse's rump. He felt his feet being tied so that he'd be unable to turn around before reaching town.

When all was done, Diamond said, "Give each of 'em a cut across the rump."

Bondy threw a last glance at Martha Lansing, standing in the door. He tried to make his glance reassuring but he knew it didn't quite come off. Someone gave his horse a cut across the rump with the end of a rope and the horse broke into a gallop, his hooves throwing up huge clods of mud as he thundered up the lane. DeVoe's horse, similarly struck, followed not far behind. A couple of the clods thrown up by Bondy's horse struck DeVoe on the back.

Bondy had always prided himself on being able to control himself. He had a temper, of course, but rarely did he let it show. And never had it gained control of him.

But now he could feel it rising in a way it never had before. Diamond's final act had demonstrated what utter and complete contempt he had for the law. His earlier actions should have revealed it to Bondy, he realized now. His burning of Mike Logan's livery barn and house, his taking over Martha Lansing's house and holding her prisoner, his threat that he would hunt Mike down like a wolf and kill him like one—these things should have warned Bondy and he should have brought a posse out here with him.

But he wasn't used to such massive lawbreaking in his county. Since he'd been sheriff, he'd mostly served papers and arrested drunks. Occasionally he'd broken up a fight and once he'd jailed an itinerant cowboy for breaking into Seward's Store to steal some food. Seward had declined to prosecute.

DeVoe called, "We're sure going to look like a pair of fools!"

"We are a pair of fools. I should have taken a posse out there after him."

"What are we going to do now?"

"Get into town and get untied. Then I'll get up a posse and go out there after him."

"He's got Martha and her kids."

"He won't . . ." Bondy had been about to say that Diamond wouldn't hurt either Martha or her kids. But suddenly he wasn't sure. Diamond had called her a whore. He would have blasted both him and DeVoe if they hadn't done what he ordered them to. Diamond was out of his head and completely unpredictable. And if he happened to lose any more of his sons . . .

Bondy faced the truth. Jasper Diamond was a mad dog and ought to be treated like one. Helplessly Bondy sat, facing his horse's rump, unable even to strike the horse and make him travel faster toward town.

Eventually they reached the outskirts of the town. The first man who saw them immediately rushed over and cut the ropes binding them. Bondy, by now raging, said in a tightly controlled voice, "Go ring the fire bell. I want a posse to go after Jasper Diamond and his men."

He and DeVoe had both dismounted and then remounted properly. They rode to the jail. Bondy got himself a double-barreled shotgun and a rifle and plenty of shells for each. DeVoe got himself a rifle and revolver. He stuck the revolver down into his coat pocket and shoved the rifle into his saddle boot.

Then both of them mounted and rode to the church. People, curious, had begun to gather, but Bondy waited until there were twenty-five or thirty before he mounted the church steps and spoke to them. He said, "Jasper Diamond has taken over Martha Lansing's place and has put out word he'll burn her out unless Mike Logan gives himself up. He tied Sid and me and sent us back to town, looking back instead of forward. He's flaunted the law and I want a posse to arrest him and bring him back to jail."

People on the edge of the crowd began to move away. Someone said, "Maybe Diamond's right. I've always wondered how Martha Lansing made a living in that damn little cabin out there."

Bondy called some names, the names of men nearest him. Behind him, others began to melt away. Bondy said, "Get horses and guns and be down at the jail in twenty minutes."

The men looked at one another. Then, as if by common signal, they shook their heads.

Bondy knew he had lost. He had the power to charge anyone who refused to join a posse, but in practice it didn't work. If men refused to go, they couldn't be forced, and if they were brought to trial for their refusal, a jury of local citizens always turned them loose. Which left the sheriff helpless unless the citizens were willing to go with him.

He uttered a single, disgusted, obscene word. Two or three of the men stared at him angrily. They all turned, though, and left the church.

Bondy didn't know what the hell he was going to do now. If Mike Logan showed up in town before he went out to Martha Lansing's place, maybe the three of them could get together. Three against four wasn't very good odds, particularly when the four held three hostages, but it looked like that was the only alternative they had left.

Disgustedly he looked at Sid DeVoe. "Let's go back to the office."

Riding back, he glanced aside at Sid DeVoe, wondering whether Sid was going to quit him too. If he did, it would be him and Mike Logan against Diamond and all three of his men, with the lives of Martha Lansing and her two children as the stakes.

He thought bitterly that when this was over he was going to get some other kind of job. People elected you to uphold their laws and protect them. But when the going got rough, they wanted to quit you cold. Well, to hell with them. Next term they could get another man.

CHAPTER FIFTEEN

Mike rode away from the Castillo ranch, aware that he was making trail that could easily be followed by anyone. Where there wasn't drifted snow, there was mud.

He had no idea where he could go now. He *should* just continue riding north and leave the country for good. He could send for Martha and she would come. But they would be destitute and he was damned if he was going to start his life with her that way. Not when all he'd done was protect her from an attacker in her own home. Not when he'd shot that attacker only after he'd been shot himself. Not when he'd had a thriving business and she'd had a house, both filled with possessions they valued and would have difficulty replacing.

He was damned if he was going to give Diamond that much satisfaction. Hell, Jasper Diamond wasn't God. He was supposed to abide by the law just the same as everybody else.

But what else to do? He glanced toward the northwest, from which direction any more storms would come, and for an instant hope rushed through him. There were low clouds over the land to the northwest, where the moun-

tains were, and they weren't the puffy, white thun-
derclouds of summer. They were the low-lying, dark gray
clouds that promised another winter storm.

That kind of storm would be the best thing that could
happen to him, Mike realized. The ground would freeze
and would again be covered with blowing, drifting snow.
He could move about at will, limited only by his own
ability or lack of it to keep from getting lost. But how
long would that storm take getting here? Right now the
clouds appeared to be a least twenty or thirty miles away.
Upon their speed depended a lot of things, including,
maybe, his life.

There was a five-hundred-dollar reward on him, which
cut down drastically the number of people he could trust.
The Egans would have turned him in for it. Except for
Rosita, so would the Castillos. Any solitary rider that
sighted him would try to shoot him down for it.

He found himself riding south instead of north. The
odds of survival were bad riding south, but then, hell,
they'd never been good ever since he'd shot Reese Diamond. They weren't any worse now than they had been
then.

He saw the man coming from a long way off, just a
speck riding along the road, which Mike himself had not
yet reached.

Immediately he put his horses down into a gully that
led toward the road. He kicked the saddle horse into a
trot and the packhorse kept pace. Mike couldn't know
whether the rider had seen him, but he didn't think he
had.

The gulch led to within two hundred yards of the road,

then flattened out. Mike left his horses where they could not be seen from the road, and continued on foot. He found a place where the road went over a rise, and waited at its crest, crouched so that the rider wouldn't see him before he was ready to be seen.

When he saw the rider's head appear above the rise, he got to his feet, rifle cocked and at his shoulder, aimed straight at the man now recognizable as Russ Gargan. He said, "Don't stop. Just come on at the same gait you're traveling now."

For a moment, he thought Gargan was going to bolt. He shifted his point of aim from Gargan's chest to his horse's belly. But Gargan changed his mind. He came on, giving his shoulders a slight shrug. "The boss sent me out with a message for you. I'd just as well give it to you in person as to have somebody else pass it along."

"What's the message?"

"He's at Martha Lansing's house."

"He hasn't hurt her?" Fury blazed suddenly and uncontrolled in Mike.

"She's all right. He don't intend hurting her or the kids. But if you don't turn yourself in to him, he's going to burn her house and everything else she's got. And he's going to leave her and the kids out there to get to town the best way they can."

Mike glanced quickly over his shoulder at the pile of dark gray clouds. The storm was coming fast. It might hit before he could even reach Martha Lansing's place. This time of year when a storm came down out of the north it came swiftly and struck like the last one had, with ferocious intensity. He asked, "How long's he going to wait?"

"Until he gets tired of waiting, I suppose."

Mike said, "Get off your horse."

Gargan glanced at the approaching pile of clouds. "You can't leave me out here without a horse. That goddamn storm will be here before I can walk back to Martha Lansing's place. I'll freeze to death."

Mike repeated evenly, shifting the muzzle of his rifle ever so slightly, "Get off your horse."

Gargan obeyed. He got off on the wrong side, away from Mike. Mike fired instantly. The bullet passed several inches over Gargan's head. Mike said, "Get around here where I can see you."

Gargan turned his horse until he was between Mike and the horse. There was no gun in his hands but he had obviously been trying to get a hand underneath his coat.

A slight breeze began to blow out of the north, cooler than the sun-warmed air. Mike walked over and took the reins of Russ Gargan's horse. He said, "Start walking. I'll leave your horse tied a couple of miles down the road. But before you do, unbutton your coat and drop that gun."

Gargan unbuttoned his coat, fumbled with his gunbelt, then let it drop.

"Step away from it and start walking."

Scowling, Gargan did. Mike picked up the gun and belt, mounted, and rode back to where he had left his own two horses. He withdrew the rifle from Gargan's saddle boot and threw it into a snowdrift along with Gargan's revolver and belt. He dismounted from Gargan's horse and tied the reins to his own packhorse's tail. Then he mounted his own saddle horse and climbed him out of the gully.

He could see Gargan trudging along toward town. Glancing behind, he could almost see the cloudbank move, so swift was its approach. A couple of hours, he guessed, at most. He kicked his horse into a trot.

He left Gargan behind, riding a distance he guessed Gargan could walk in two hours if he walked fast. Then he dismounted, untied the reins of Gargan's horse from his packhorse's tail, and tied Gargan's horse at the side of the road to a clump of brush.

Gargan would be two hours behind him reaching Martha Lansing's place and Gargan would be unarmed. Besides that, by the time Gargan arrived the matter ought to be resolved, one way or another. Mike had no idea how he was going to cope with Diamond and his men in possession of Martha Lansing's place but he knew he had to figure something out.

He tried to estimate how many of them there were. Jasper Diamond himself. One or two crewmen at least. And two of his sons. Four or five men against one. And they would be in Martha Lansing's house, shooting from cover, with three hostages in case anything went wrong.

With his thoughts churning, he headed along the road, trying to figure out something that would turn the tables and give him a chance.

Behind him, the storm rolled southward, the clouds building up higher and higher as the storm drew near. An hour passed. Another. The wind was blowing steadily now straight out of the north, and, as it had the other day, the temperature began dropping rapidly.

But now, knowing that the storm would strike before he reached Martha's place, he knew how he was going to handle this. What he had to do was draw them away from her house, pursuing him. Trying to battle them there was idiocy bordering on suicide, and put Martha and her kids in too much jeopardy.

The storm would give him some chance of escape. And it would draw them away from her house. Maybe, just maybe, he could pick them off one by one before they shot him down. But if they did shoot him down, Diamond would probably be satisfied. He wouldn't return to Martha Lansing's house. He wouldn't burn her out because there would no longer be any satisfaction in it for him.

By now the sky was half covered with clouds. Two hours after he left Gargan afoot, they obscured the sun, and not long after that, small, stinging particles of sleet filled the air.

Already the ground was beginning to freeze. The tracks of Mike's horses were less and less plain the nearer to Martha's place he got.

Finally, in mid-afternoon, he reached the place he needed to turn off if he was to escape being seen. Circling, keeping a low rise between himself and the house, he left the road. He went as far as the creek, and tied his horses there, his saddle horse to a tree, his packhorse's halter rope tied to the saddlehorn. Then, afoot, he worked his way carefully down the creek until, through the trees, he could see Martha Lansing's house and the shed and corral in which she kept her cows.

Smoke issued from the chimney, blown instantly away,

horizontally, by the rising wind. Mike hoped this storm
wasn't going to be as bad as the last, even as he turned up
the collar of his sheepskin coat and pulled his hat lower
on his head so that the wind couldn't snatch it off.

Several horses were in the corral. He counted four. All
wore saddles, perhaps with the cinches loosened, but in
readiness.

Four men, then. Previously there had been six, but Diamond
had probably sent one to town and sent Gargan out
to the ranches trying to get word to Mike as to what he
intended to do to Martha's house unless Mike surrendered
himself.

Mike crept along the ground cautiously, on hands and
knees, his rifle in his hand. Finally he reached a thick
clump of brush that he thought would pretty effectively
screen him from the house. He poked his rifle through so
that he could shoot if he wanted to without having the
bullet deflected by a branch.

The air continued to grow colder, but it was already
obvious that this storm was not going to be as severe as
the last. It was not as cold, for one thing. The snow was
not coming down as thickly, for another. But the snow
was thick enough—thick enough to hide Mike when he
had to flee; and the ground was frozen hard enough that
it would leave no tracks. Only where there was accumulated
snow would the tracks of his two horses show, and
following trail would slow down Diamond and his men
enough to give Mike a chance to stay ahead of them, despite
the fact that his horses were tired and those of Diamond's
men were not.

Despite his warm coat, he began to chill. His shoulder,

held in such an awkward position, began to ache again. He shifted position, trying to ease the ache, but it did little good.

Sooner or later, someone had to come out of the house. But how long would it be? The air grew colder, the snow thicker as the moments passed. And as time wore on, the sky began to grow darker.

Silently, helplessly, Mike cursed to himself. If it got dark before he got his chance, they probably wouldn't chase him at all. If that happened, he didn't know what he'd do. They'd threaten Martha and her kids and he'd have no choice but to surrender himself.

But even while he was thinking these thoughts, the house door opened and a man came out. He headed for the outhouse.

Mike couldn't tell who it was in the gloomy light and driving snow but he did know it wasn't one of Diamond's sons. He didn't want to kill the man, but shooting in this kind of light was chancy to say the least and he'd just have to do his best.

He drew as good a bead as he could, aiming at the man's moving legs. He squeezed the trigger carefully.

Even as he did, his elbow, resting on the ground, slipped ever so slightly in the snow. His point of aim raised slightly as the rifle boomed.

The man pitched forward, as though struck violently from behind. Immediately the door of the house was flung open and three men came plunging out. One was Diamond. One was Rudy. The third was Hugo.

Mike could have shot any one of them. But he knew that if he did, the other two would duck back inside and then Martha and her kids would suffer for what he had done.

So instead, he got to his feet, not trying to avoid noise, not trying to avoid being seen. He ran toward the place where his horses were concealed.

Behind him he heard Jasper Diamond roar, "There he is! There's the sonofabitch! Get your horses and get after him. This time I want that bastard caught!"

CHAPTER SIXTEEN

A few shots were fired at him before he went out of sight in the brush. One clipped a twig above his head. None of the others came close.

He didn't waste time making sure they all were following. He knew they would. Diamond didn't really care about Martha Lansing or her kids. What Diamond wanted was Mike. Martha had never been more to him than a means of getting Mike to come to him.

Well, Mike thought, now he had them after him. Three of them at least. Gargan wouldn't get back in time to join the chase and there was a good chance Diamond had sent someone else to town with the same message Gargan had been carrying.

He'd shot one between the cabin and the outhouse, probably Tubbs. If Diamond had indeed sent a man to town, then only three were now pursuing him.

Careless of the noise, because he wanted them to think they were gaining on him, he spurred his horse through the dense underbrush that lined the creek. Almost immediately it became apparent to him that he wasn't going to make it trailing a packhorse, so he dropped the pack animal's halter rope. Afterward he rode up out of the creek bottom and, when he reached higher ground, glanced behind.

Diamond, unmistakable because of his size, was climbing his lunging horse up out of the creek bottom. Hugo and Rudy came on close behind. The three were no more than about four hundred yards away.

Mike knew that he had made a mistake. He should have cut them down, one by one, as they came out the door of Martha Lansing's little house. He should have been as ruthless as Diamond was, and if he had, he wouldn't be in such a precarious position now. His horse was tired, having been ridden hard for almost three days. The mounts Diamond and his sons were riding were undoubtedly fresh. He might be able to stay ahead of them for a while, but in the end they'd catch him. When they did, they'd kill him with as little hesitation as they'd feel stepping on a bug.

But the wind was picking up, and it was mid-afternoon. If the storm hit soon, maybe he could stay ahead of them until dark. It was, he realized, the only chance he had.

He therefore held his horse to a steady lope, glancing behind often to make sure they did not gain on him too fast. Apparently Diamond was satisfied, for the present at least, to keep pace, knowing his three horses were fresh and Mike's was tired. He could afford to wait because the end was sure.

Mike tried to decide what he was going to do. Continued flight was foolish and useless. Sooner or later he'd be caught, or he'd have to stop and fight it out. Of the two alternatives, the second was the only one that was palatable. And if he was going to stop and fight, then he'd better find a place from which he *could* fight effectively before they closed the gap and it was too late.

A gulch, he thought. If he could find a gulch, and if he could get his horse into it without hesitation at its edge, and if he could be off the horse instantly and back to the lip of the gulch before the pursuers reached it . . .

Too many ifs, he thought. Too many things had to be perfect before it would work at all.

Maybe he was really going to die out here today. Maybe he had never had a chance against as formidable an adversary as Diamond. Then he thought of Reese. He thought of Lentz, one-legged now. He thought of Hank in jail and of the crewmen he had either killed or hurt. And all he had himself was a shoulder wound, which, despite the trouble it was giving him, was superficial and would quickly heal.

Suddenly, so unexpectedly that he was thrown from his saddle, his horse went into a broad, deep wash that had, two days ago, drifted so completely full of snow that the sun hadn't melted it. The horse floundered helplessly, frightened and trying to reach the other side. Mike, fully aware of those pursuing him, fought his way back to the edge of the gulch. He had been planning for something like this, and therefore had his rifle in his hand. All he could hope was that the fall hadn't jammed the barrel full of snow. If it had, the gun would blow up in his face.

He could see the triumphant expression on Diamond's face, so close was the man by now. He fired, his sights on Diamond's chest, but so uncertain was his footing in the deep snow that his bullet missed, striking the chest of Diamond's horse instead.

The horse went down, throwing Diamond to within a dozen yards of the edge of the wash. His falling seemed to unnerve his sons, and the two hauled their horses to a momentary halt.

In an instant, Mike knew, they'd get over their surprise and begin firing at him. He took a quick bead on Rudy's horse, fired, and saw the horse go down. Hugo, believing himself to be the only one left, immediately whirled his horse and galloped out of range.

Now Mike moved quickly. Diamond, half stunned, was stirring and would soon be up, bellowing orders to his sons. Rudy's leg was pinned temporarily underneath his horse but Diamond would be able to free him quickly enough.

Mike floundered through the deep snow in the gully to the other side. His horse was just now lunging up the far bank. Mike dropped the rifle and grabbed his tail with both hands. The horse regained level ground, with Mike clinging to his tail. Instantly Mike released it, ran ahead and seized the horse's reins, then swung to his back, keeping the horse between him and Jasper Diamond for as long as he could.

Diamond was already firing as fast as he could work the lever of his rifle, and Hugo, having returned, was firing too, but both of them were too excited and too anxious to take careful aim. Not one of their bullets touched either Mike or his horse.

He kicked the horse in the sides and the frightened animal broke into a lope. In seconds, Mike left the bitterly cursing trio behind.

Now, he assessed what had been done. He had lost his rifle, and he regretted that, but if he hadn't dropped it and seized his horse's tail with both hands, he might still be back in that snow-filled gulch. As far as hurting Diamond and his sons, he hadn't, except to put two of them afoot. Two could ride their remaining horse, but not three. One would have to walk.

Or maybe one would come on, continuing the pursuit, while the others went back afoot for more horses and more help.

He had pulled his horse back to a trot as soon as he was comfortably out of rifle range. He went over a ridge and disappeared, but he turned and came back, letting only the top of his head show above the ridge.

Down there, now half a mile away, Diamond was having a violent argument with his sons. Finishing it, he put bullets into the necks of the two downed horses, which were still struggling on the ground. Then he mounted and motioned for one of his sons to get up behind.

He looked back once, but Mike doubted if Diamond saw him, because only the upper half of his head was showing above the ridge. Then Diamond rode back the way he had come, with one son sullenly trudging along behind.

Mike briefly considered going back down after they had gone and trying to recover his rifle from the deep gully snow. He abandoned the idea. A storm was coming up and it was getting late. He wasn't likely to find the gun because it probably had gone too deep into the snow.

Frowning, he turned his horse and went north again.
Diamond would go back to Martha's place. He had ac-
complished nothing, except to make Diamond more furious, if that was possible, than before. The loss of two
horses meant nothing to Diamond. The loss of Tubbs
meant little more, because he could always hire men.

Mike silently cursed himself for not having been ruthless enough. Then he realized that he was blaming himself unfairly. He *had* drawn a bead on Diamond's chest,
knowing Jasper Diamond's death would end this whole
brutal business. It was the softness of the snow beneath
him that had made him miss.

Well, it was done, and he'd just as well make the best
of it. He just hoped Diamond didn't go back and burn
Martha Lansing's house to satisfy his rage.

What he needed, Mike admitted at last, was help. He
needed the sheriff's help and he needed the help of the
sheriff's deputy, Sid DeVoe.

Diamond might not go back to Martha's place. At least
not right away. Maybe he'd go to town to try to hire more
men and to get more horses and supplies.

In any case, Mike didn't dare go into town himself and
try to see the sheriff or DeVoe. There was too much
chance he'd run into Diamond, or one of his sons or one
of his men. Or run into someone that wanted the five-
hundred-dollar reward badly enough to try to kill him.

Who could he get to take the sheriff a message? he
wondered. Who could he trust to go to town for him?

Not Egan or Castillo, certainly. Suddenly his mind settled on a man he could trust. John Farnham. He wondered why he hadn't thought of Farnham before.

Snow fell steadily, blowing on a chill north wind, but neither as thick nor as cold as it had been a couple of days ago. Mike turned his horse and headed toward Farnham's place.

Farnham was a middle-aged, solid man, bearded, who always dressed in faded bib overalls and wide-brimmed straw hat. He had no cattle, except for a few milk cows, but he had a wide meadow that was naturally irrigated by a stream that flowed down through the middle of it, and he put up about four hundred tons of hay a year, which he sold to other ranchers but not to Jasper Diamond, who raised enough of his own. His wife had a large vegetable garden and Farnham kept her supplied with venison, most of which she canned for winter use.

Farnham wouldn't give a damn about a five-hundred-dollar reward. He'd probably refuse it if it was offered to him. Mike began to feel a little hope. He could ask Farnham to go to town for him and tell the sheriff to meet him at Martha Lansing's place. If he and the sheriff and Sid DeVoe got there before Diamond returned, they'd have the advantage for once, instead of Diamond having it.

He held his horse to a steady trot. Gradually light faded from the sky. The snow still came down, but lightly, and the wind began to moderate. Mike thought about his packhorse, which he'd had to leave behind. The animal would go to town and somebody would take the packsaddle off him, he thought. But everything he needed was in the gunnysacks on that packsaddle. His food, his extra ammunition, his blanket roll. Furthermore, Diamond knew he was now without supplies. All Diamond had to do was wait.

Having made Mike come back once, Diamond would know that he could do it again. By occupying Martha Lansing's place. Only Mike was going to fool him this time, if he had the time.

Farnham's place was a good fifteen miles from town, and six or seven miles beyond the place where Mike had shot Diamond's horse and that of one of his sons. It took Mike two hours to cover the distance because he didn't see any sense in unnecessarily tiring his already-weary horse.

At last he saw the lamplight shining from the windows of John Farnham's house. He took the road that wound along the edge of the hayfield and headed for it, hoping that his estimate of John Farnham's character was better than his estimate of Castillo's and Lester Egan's.

CHAPTER SEVENTEEN

———◆———

As Mike rode along the edge of John Farnham's hayfield, he could hear the faint but strident sound of a cowbell someplace down in the middle of the hay meadow. He could dimly see the stacks of hay Farnham had put up during the summer scattered across the huge hayfield. The ringing of the cowbell continued and Mike supposed Farnham's son, Jake, was driving in the cows to be milked.

He continued toward the house and arrived at the same time Jake arrived with the cows. Jake drove them into the barn, seven of them, without seeing Mike. Mike dismounted, tied his horse, and went to the back door. He didn't see any horses tied anyplace, and anyway he didn't see how Diamond could have beaten him here.

Mrs. Farnham answered his knock. She was a middle-aged, rather heavy woman, with a round, pleasant face that just now was flushed from the heat of the stove.

Mike knew he looked like the devil. He hadn't shaved for days. Neither had he washed. There was grease spattered over his coat collar and shoulders, and there was blood on the shoulder of his coat that had soaked through from the wound.

He said, "Hello, Mrs. Farnham. It's Mike Logan."

"Well, come in." She stood aside and Mike went into the steaming hot kitchen. John Farnham was sitting at the kitchen table, smoking a pipe. He got up immediately and helped Mike off with his coat. "You've been shot!"

"Reese shot me."

"We heard Diamond was looking for you but we didn't hear you had been shot. We heard he burned your livery stable and your house and offered a five-hundred-dollar reward for you. You ought to go to the sheriff. Diamond is not the law."

Mike said, "That's why I came here."

Mrs. Farnham said, "Never mind all that now. You need something to eat. I can tell that by looking at you. And I know you'd like to wash."

She got a basin and poured hot water into it from the teakettle on the stove. She put in enough cold with a dipper so that it wouldn't be too hot, then gave it to him. Farnham carried a lamp out onto the screened-in back porch and Mike carried out the pan. He washed his face and hands and ran a comb through his hair. He felt better after doing so but he was ravenously hungry. He went back into the kitchen, with John Farnham following.

Farnham was a couple of inches shorter than Mike, thickset with a chest that was strong and deep. He said, "You need me to help?"

Mike nodded. "First, let me tell you all of it. I don't know how much you've heard." Mike then related the full story of his misadventures.

"What do you want me to do?" Farnham asked when Mike had finished.

"Go to town and tell the sheriff to go out to Martha's place, along with Sid DeVoe. I don't dare go to town, with a reward on me dead or alive. Tell Bondy I'll meet him there."

"All right. I can do that."

Farnham's son, Jake, came in, carrying two brimming buckets of milk. He put them on a stand on the back porch. Mrs. Farnham said, "Let the milk go until later, Jake. We're going to eat right away."

Jake came into the kitchen and sat down. Mike sat down beside him and Farnham sat across the table. Mrs. Farnham began putting on the food.

Mike was ravenous and wolfed his food, even though he tried to eat as slowly as he could. He was finished long before the others were, but he refused more food, knowing he'd be a lot better off if he didn't eat too much. He didn't know how much longer he was going to be on the run.

Farnham got up when he had finished. "I'll be going."

Mike asked, "Can you loan me a rifle? I lost mine in that gully, and I had to leave my packhorse, so I haven't even got extra ammunition for my revolver."

"Sure. But I don't think I've got more than a half a dozen shells for it." Farnham left the room and returned soon after with a carbine and a small handful of shells. There were seven.

Jake kept watching Mike, but whenever Mike would meet his glance, Jake would look away. They all got up from the table and Mike thanked Mrs. Farnham for the meal. Farnham went out to saddle a horse. Mike started to follow him.

Jake asked, "Where are you going now?"

Mike glanced at him. Jake didn't have the same solid look to him that his father did. Mike said, "Back to Martha Lansing's place, I guess. I doubt if Diamond went back there after I shot two of his horses. He probably either went home or to town to get more. Maybe he'll try hiring more men, or he might raise the reward."

He went out. The elder Farnham had already saddled a horse. He said, "I'll ride part of the way with you."

Mike nodded. He mounted and fell in beside Farnham as the man took the road leading along the edge of the big hayfield. Mike held his horse to a trot, and Farnham kept pace. Mike figured they probably had all night. He also knew that, or maybe felt, it might take that long.

———◆———

Jake Farnham went out on the porch and saw his father and Mike ride away.

He strained the milk into the separator, then opened the cream can and placed it under one spout, a bucket under the other. He began to turn the crank.

He could hear his mother moving around in the kitchen, picking up the table, getting water ready to do the dishes.

Jake knew that someday this ranch would belong to him. Theirs was the best and biggest hayfield in the county. The place would give him as good a living as it had his father and mother for all the years they'd lived here. The trouble was, Jake didn't want it. He didn't want to spend his life milking cows, cutting and stacking hay, building and repairing fences, doing all the things he and his father spent their time doing now.

There was more to life than this little plot of land, no matter how productive or beautiful it might be. There was a whole world out there, with mountains and oceans and big cities and railroads and sailing ships. Jake didn't know what he wanted to do once he got away from here. He only knew he had to get away.

The trouble, and he was ashamed whenever he admitted it to himself, was that he was afraid. Other boys might run away with nothing in their pockets but Jake didn't have the courage for it. What if he couldn't find a job? He could think of half a hundred terrifying possibilities, things that might happen to him unless he had some money to get started on.

Besides, even if nothing happened, he wouldn't be able to see the world. He'd have to take a job someplace to support himself and there he'd stay, stuck to that job just like he was stuck to this.

He thought about the reward Diamond had offered for Mike Logan. Five hundred dollars. It was more, he supposed, than his father had ever possessed. It was enough to buy a farm, a house, a business, anything he might want to buy. But it was also something else. It was a ticket to all the things in the world that he wanted to see. You could go around the world on five hundred dollars. You could live for a year. He could see the things he wanted to see and decide what he really wanted to do with his life.

Briefly, but only briefly, he considered what Diamond would do to Mike once he got his hands on him. Then, firmly, he put that thought from his mind. Mike had killed Reese Diamond, old man Diamond's son, hadn't he? And who was to say whether Mike's story about what had happened was really true? Besides, he reasoned, if he didn't turn Mike in to Diamond and collect the reward, somebody else would. One way or another, Mike Logan was going to be caught.

He finished separating the cream, put the lid on the can, then carried the two buckets of skim milk outside. They had a few pigs and he poured both buckets into the pigs' trough. Normally, now, he would have gone back to the house and carried the buckets and the parts of the cream separator in for his mother to wash. But not tonight.

Glancing guiltily at the house, he went into the barn and saddled his own horse. He led the horse out and down the road a way before he mounted him. Then he kicked the horse's sides, forcing him into a steady lope.

It wasn't hard to make the horse maintain the gait. He'd been in the barn for several days and he wanted to run. Jake headed him straight for Diamond's place, from here less than four miles away across country. Diamond's was about six miles from Martha Lansing's place. If Jake loped all the way to Diamond's, and if Diamond loped his horses all the way to Martha Lansing's, they'd probably reach it before Mike Logan or the sheriff could. In darkness, Diamond ought to be able to take Mike easily enough when he arrived. He ought to be able to do it without firing a shot. At least that was what Jake Farnham told himself.

The storm had settled down into the average kind of

early winter snow that bothered nobody. The snowfall was light, the wind moderate. Even in darkness, landmarks were visible and there wasn't enough snow on the ground yet to make traveling difficult.

Several times during the four-mile ride to Diamond's, Jake had second thoughts. What would his father say when he learned that his son had turned in Mike Logan for the reward? What would his mother say?

Angrily he told himself it didn't matter what they said. He would get the reward and go. Diamond, if he got Mike Logan tonight, would probably pay the reward to-morrow. He could leave right away. Maybe he wouldn't even have to tell his father and mother he was going or that he was paying for his trip with the reward.

These kinds of thoughts depressed him in spite of himself. So he put them aside and began to think of all the places he would go and all the things he was going to do.

He brought Diamond's buildings into sight and entered the long lane lined on both sides by tall poplar trees, their leaves now golden, blowing some as the wind tore them off the trees.

Here, Jake stopped his horse. What if, after turning Mike Logan in, he didn't even get the reward? What if Diamond already knew Mike would go back to Martha Lansing's place and was already headed there himself? He'd be known all over the country as a Judas and he wouldn't even have anything to show for it.

But there were lights in the house down there. There were horses saddled and ready in the yard.

He rode on down the lane, and as he approached the

house, a man called, "Hold it, mister! Who are you and what do you want?"

"It's Jake Farnham. I want to see Mr. Diamond."

"What about? He's a busy man."

"It's about Mike Logan. I know where he is."

"Well, get down and come on in!"

Jake got down and the man escorted him into the house. Jasper Diamond was there, along with Rudy and Hugo, his two remaining sons. Also present was Wong, the cook, and the old choreman, Gebhardt. Harrison was also here, and there were three new men that Jake had never seen before, one of whom had brought him in.

Even without the cook, that made eight. Diamond picked up his coat and put it on. He crammed his hat down on his head and put on his chaps. Diamond looked at Jake. "You know where Logan is?"

"Will I get the reward?"

"If we catch him where you say he is, you will."

"He just left our place. He got pa to go after the sheriff and his deputy. They were to meet him at Mrs. Lansing's place. That's where Mike Logan's heading now. I figure if you ride hard, you can get there before he does, because his horse is pretty tired."

Diamond nodded. "All right, kid. If we get him, you get the reward. I was going there anyway, but not that fast. We'd have gotten there after he and the sheriff had time to dig in."

Jake hesitated. The other men were already hurrying out the door. Finally he asked, "Can I stay here until it's over with?"

Diamond gave him a long, hard look. "You want the money but you don't like the Judas part. Right?"

Jake felt his face begin to burn. But he didn't have to reply. With a contemptuous snort, Diamond went out the door, slamming it behind. A few moments later, Jake heard the pound of horses' hooves on the hard-packed ground.

Wong had gone back into the kitchen. There was only one lamp burning in here. Jake sat down uncomfortably on one of the leather-covered chairs. He wondered where Mrs. Diamond was.

CHAPTER EIGHTEEN

Mike Logan rode with Farnham for about two miles, just beyond the end of the hayfield. He didn't know why, but he felt uneasy. He kept remembering the way Jake Farnham had looked at him whenever he wasn't looking at Jake, and the way young Farnham had always quickly looked away whenever he did.

His uneasiness continued to deepen. Once, he considered asking John Farnham if he thought his son was capable of turning him in to Diamond, and then he discarded the idea. Farnham was helping him, and questioning Farnham's son would be insulting him.

But the uneasiness persisted. At last, still less than three miles from Farnham's house, he said, "John, do you mind trading horses with me? I think I ought to get to Martha's place right away. I don't know why, but I feel damned uneasy about her."

"Sure. You can have my horse." Farnham dismounted and, when Mike had dismounted, exchanged reins with him. Mike had the feeling Farnham was smiling in the darkness as he said, "Pretty fond of her, aren't you?"

"I asked her to marry me, and she said yes. If I can get Diamond off my back."

"Go ahead, then. I'll send Bondy and DeVoe out."

Mike thanked him and swung to the back of Farnham's horse. He immediately kicked the horse into a lope. It was neither too dark nor was the snow too thick to see landmarks, and he set a course straight for Martha Lansing's house. When possible, he forced the horse to run. At other times, he let him lope. Only when the ground was very rough or cut with deep gulches did he slow the animal to a trot.

He felt nearly helpless. He had lost his own rifle and all the extra ammunition he had been carrying for it. All he had was Farnham's rifle, with seven shells, and his revolver, which contained only five.

Farnham's horse, which had been fresh and eager to run at first, began to tire. But Mike was closing the distance between him and Martha's house rapidly. He wasn't going to ruin Farnham's horse, but neither was he going to spare him any more than he thought necessary.

About a mile short of Martha's house, his course brought him into the road that ran between Martha's and Diamond's place. He stopped for an instant where there was light snow lying on it, and stared down, looking for hoof prints. There weren't any, not even old ones drifted over. He went on, again kicking the horse into a lope. He still wasn't safe. Diamond could have gone to town instead of home for horses and more men. He could still have beaten Mike back to Martha's house.

He reached the lane leading to Martha's house. Here,

again, he stared down at the road, looking for tracks. Once more he failed to find them.

Lamplight glowed from the windows of the house. But still Mike didn't ride straight in. He circled the house until he reached the heavy brush along the creek. He tied Farnham's horse and moved in toward the cabin afoot.

No horses were visible in the yard and there just wasn't any place horses could be hidden except in the shed where Martha kept her cows. And if the cows had been driven out to make room for horses, they'd be somewhere around bawling their heads off.

Reassured, Mike approached the house and peered into a window. He saw Martha at the stove. He saw Tubbs lying on a couch, his eyes closed, his upper body bare, with a bandage wound around it. The bandage had a hand-sized spot of blood on it. Diamond had left him here and Martha was taking care of him. At least Mike hadn't killed the man, and that was a relief.

Now, feeling safe, but holding the rifle ready, he knocked on Martha's door. He heard her footsteps crossing the room and her soft call, "Who is it?"

"It's Mike."

She opened the door at once and came into his arms. Without releasing her, he pushed her on inside and kicked the door closed behind him. "Nobody here but him?"

"That's all. Everybody left to chase you as soon as you shot him. They haven't come back yet."

"How is he? Is he hurt bad?"

"He's shot through the chest. I think if he could be gotten to the doctor, he might be all right. But Mr. Diamond didn't even seem to be listening when I told him the man needed the doctor right away."

Mike put Farnham's rifle down against the wall beside the door. He grinned at Frank and Julie, staring big-eyed at him from the bedroom door. He asked, "Did he have any guns? Or ammunition?"

"He did, but Diamond took them."

"What about you? Have you got a gun?"

"Just that old muzzle-loader."

"Have you got powder, ball, and caps for it?"

She said, "I've got some things that go with it. I'll get them for you."

She brought the gun, which was nearly six feet long, and a small pouch and powder horn. In the pouch, Mike found bullets and caps. He said, "Get me a rag."

She did, and, removing the ramrod attached to the gun, Mike began to load it. He poured a measure of powder in first, followed it with a patch of rag, then the heavy .50-caliber bullet. Lastly he pressed a cap onto the rusty nipple. This gun would give him one more shot, if it worked at all. He placed the gun beside Farnham's rifle at the side of the door.

Martha asked worriedly, "Do you think they're coming back?"

"I'm sure they are." He didn't say anything about his suspicions of young Farnham. He said, "They want me and they know that threatening you is the best way to get to me."

"But you're here first. Doesn't that give you an advantage?"

"It would if I had ammunition. Farnham's gone to town

after Bondy and DeVoe. In the meantime, I think we
ought to blow out the lamps and barricade this place the
best we can. Does Tubbs need anything that you can't do
for him in the dark?"

She shook her head. "He's either unconscious or asleep.
I've done all I can for him."

"All right then. Blow out the lamps." To the two children he said, "We're going to play a game. There's going
to be a lot of noise after a while and I want you two to
get under the bed when it happens. And stay there, no
matter what. Can you do that?"

The pair nodded solemnly at him. Mike blew out the
last lamp.

To Martha he whispered softly, "The log walls will stop
most of the bullets. But they can still come in the windows or through the door. I want you with the children
when the shooting starts."

"Can't I help . . . ?"

He said, "If there was plenty of ammunition, I'd say
yes. But with every shot counting, I can't take a chance
on someone who might miss."

That wasn't strictly true. Martha was competent
enough to shoot a gun. He just didn't want her anyplace
where she might be hit.

He made sure the door was securely barred, then
pushed the table over against it. He went to the nearest
window and stared out at the snowy night, with Martha
standing close beside him. "How soon do you think they'll
come?"

"Soon." He felt nothing but relief that, at last, it was

going to end. He was holed up here and couldn't get away. They'd come, and when it was over, either Diamond would be dead or he would.

Now that there was nothing to do but wait, he carefully shrugged out of his heavy sheepskin coat, wincing with the pain in his shoulder as he did. He threw it on a chair and threw his hat on top of it.

He unbuckled his chaps and took them off. He felt as if he'd never had a bath and his whiskers were so long they itched. He was more tired than he had ever been in his life before and his shoulder pained him so fiercely that he knew there was infection in it. He didn't even know how he'd be able to stand the pain of a gun firing in his hands, but he knew he had to.

By feel, he made his way past the children and into the bedroom. The bed was against the wall, and there was no way a bullet fired from a distance through the bedroom window could hit anybody under it. The only danger to Martha and the kids, then, was from bullets coming in the front door or the front windows.

He returned to Martha beside the window. "Have you got any trunks?"

"Two. They're full of clothes and things."

"Where are they?"

She led the way to the trunks. With her help, he dragged them in front of the bed so that they'd protect those under it.

Now he was ready as he'd ever be, he thought. Peering out into the darkness, wanting nothing more than to be able to lie down and sleep 'round the clock, he waited, for movement, for anything that would tell him Diamond and his men were here.

———————◆———————

Diamond led his men out from the ranch at a steady lope. Pounding along behind him were Hugo and Rudy, Gebhardt, the old choreman, who might or might not be any good when the showdown came. There were also Harrison and the three new men who had ridden into the ranch this afternoon looking for winter jobs.

Diamond didn't know how much good they were going to be, either. He had told them only what he wanted them to know, that they were going after the man who had murdered one of his sons, crippled another, and burned his barn.

Expecting no more than twenty-five-dollar-a-month winter jobs feeding cattle and repairing fences, the men had eagerly accepted Diamond's promise of a hundred dollars as soon as Mike Logan was run to earth, plus thirty a month for the rest of the winter.

Maybe they'd balk at what he meant to do if he couldn't get Mike out any other way. But by then it would be too late to make any difference.

Diamond had said he'd hunt Mike down like a wolf. Now, that was what he was about to do. He'd surround the den of the bitch wolf and her pups. And when the old dog wolf showed up, he'd shoot him down. Afterward he'd do to the bitch wolf and her cubs just what he'd done to Mike. He'd burn her house, if necessary with her and her kids inside. Then and only then would Reese and Lentz be avenged.

The last few days, with their frustrations and help-
lessness, had changed Diamond from an arrogant but
otherwise fairly normal man into one who was crazy with
grief and the desire for revenge. To him, Mike Logan and
Martha Lansing had ceased being human beings and had
become animals.

To him, they were now only varmints to be exterminated the way he had always exterminated wolves, cou-
gars, and coyotes on his cattle range.

CHAPTER NINETEEN

———◆———

Mike had been waiting no more than half an hour before he heard the pound of horses' hooves upon the ground. A lot of them, he thought, riding hard. To Martha he said, "It's time. Take the kids and get under the bed."

"What about you . . . ?"

"Don't worry about me. I'm going to keep down behind the logs under the window and I'm not going to shoot unless I've got a target I can count on."

"I wish . . ."

Mike said firmly, "Go on. If not for yourself, then for the kids. Besides, if you were out here, I'd worry about you every minute of the time."

Reluctantly she crept away and he heard her talking softly with the two children in the bedroom and heard the movement of the trunks as she pushed them aside and then pulled them back into place.

A group of horsemen came to a plunging halt before the house. Mike counted eight, and wondered where Diamond had gotten that many. Diamond roared, "Logan?"

Mike didn't reply.

Diamond bawled, "Damn you, if you're in there, sing out."

Mike knew it was worth a shot. He couldn't see the sights of the rifle in this light, but he had hunted birds enough with a shotgun to be adept at pointing it. He knocked out the window with the rifle muzzle, pointed at Diamond, and fired.

He heard a howl of pain, but he didn't wait to see if he had hit Diamond or someone else. He ducked, and just in time. A fusillade of shots came from the riders bunched in the yard. The bullets took out what was left of the window glass, showering him with it, and came into the room, hitting various pieces of furniture. One clanged against the stove. Mike didn't hear any sound out of Tubbs, so he didn't guess Tubbs had been hit.

As the last shot died away, Mike risked raising his head. The horsemen were scattering, taking their horses away to tie them in the brush that lined the creek. They'd come back afoot and he probably wouldn't get another decent shot all the rest of the night.

He was no longer able to pick Diamond out of the group now that he was afoot, so he picked the next best target, pointed the rifle, and fired it again.

This time he saw the man pitch forward and lie still. He wondered who it was and whether he had killed him. He ducked down instantly again, and a second fusillade came through the window, showering him with splinters from the window frame and tiny shards of glass. One cut his face and he felt blood running from the cut.

He could hear Diamond shouting to a couple of men to take the horses and tie them where they would be safe;

and to others, to take cover and keep the house under steady fire.

Now, Mike couldn't see anything in the yard, except for the man whom he had shot. Even as he watched, the man stirred, then began to crawl away. Mike felt a touch of relief. He hadn't really wanted to kill anybody else. Except maybe for Diamond, and then only because it was the last remaining way of stopping Diamond's pursuit of him.

He wondered if Jake Farnham had betrayed him to Diamond. He hoped not. Diamond might have made his own decision to come here.

Bullets now regularly came in through the windows and the door. The other window had shattered not long after this one had. Splinters were ripped from the door and sent flying across the room every time a bullet came through. Once Mike yelled, "Tubbs is in here. He's on the bed and he can't be moved. You keep shooting like that and you're going to finish him."

The firing slackened for a moment until Diamond yelled, "Keep firing! Tubbs is already dead."

There was no way Mike could disprove that. Tubbs was unconscious and couldn't make a sound. Besides, Diamond didn't really care about Tubbs, or any of his other men for that matter. He had gone beyond caring about anything but seeing Mike Logan dead.

Now he tried to remember where all the windows were, because he knew that if he did not return their fire, they might try getting in. There was one window in the bedroom. He crawled awkwardly across the floor to the bedroom door. "All right in here?"

"We're all right." Martha's voice was trembling.

Mike could see a small square of grayish light where the window was. It was a small window, big enough to admit a man, but not without considerable difficulty, and even then the man would have to be pretty small. Mike crawled back to where Martha and the two kids were. Julie was beginning to whimper a little with fear and her mother was trying to quiet her. Mike said, "Someone could come through that window. They'll have to break it first, but keep an eye on it."

"All right. What about the windows in the other room?"

"They'd better not come in those."

Painfully he crawled back. A bullet came through one of the windows or the door about every half minute or so. Mike's shoulder was a constant burning pain now and his head felt light.

He shook his head fiercely to try to clear it as he crawled up beneath the window where he'd been before. He didn't dare weaken now. If he passed out . . . that would be the end of him, and of Martha and the kids too, probably.

He reached out, got Martha's old muzzle-loader, and pulled it to within his reach. He had five shots in Farnham's rifle, five in his revolver, and one in the muzzle-loader. He had scored solidly with one of the two bullets he'd already fired, and he had stung someone with the other one. But now all he had to shoot at was muzzle flashes, and in order to shoot at them he had to keep his head above the windowsill and risk getting one right between the eyes.

He chose a waiting game. Time was on his side. Farnham had gone to town for the sheriff and DeVoe, and they would be along eventually. Bondy might even bring a posse, which would end this once and for all.

A bullet hit Tubbs and the man grunted as it did. There was no sound afterward. Mike left his window and, carrying only his revolver in case they tried coming in the windows, crawled to where Tubbs was on the cot.

The bullet had struck him in the side and blood was running copiously from the hole. Mike laid a gentle hand on Tubbs's chest. It rose and fell shallowly a couple of times and then was still.

Anger touched Mike. He crawled back to the window and yelled, "You just killed Tubbs!"

The firing stopped. Then Diamond yelled, "He's lying. Tubbs was already shot in the chest. By him."

Mike shouted, "He'd have lived if you'd got him to the doctor!"

"You're a liar! That woman in there done everything for him the doctor could."

There was still no firing. Diamond bawled, "Keep shooting! Keep the sonofabitch busy! I know how to get him out of there!"

Mike knew how Diamond planned to get them out of there. Two sides of the house were blind. He intended to build a fire on one of those two sides. It might take the logs a while to catch but it wouldn't take the roof very long. He only hoped they could hold out until Bondy and DeVoe arrived.

The firing continued spasmodically, but Jasper Diamond could tell there were only two, maybe three guns firing. He had been headed for his horse, upon whose saddle a couple of gallon cans of coil oil hung. Now he stopped and roared angrily, "I said keep shooting! I mean all of you!"

The three new men got up from where they were lying in the brush at the edge of the clearing and came toward him. One, tall, lanky, and with a Texas drawl, said, "Don't reckon we signed on with anything like this in mind. There's a woman an' two little kids in there. An' there was one of your own crewmen, bad hurt. You let him lay there an' get killed."

"You'll get no pay . . . !"

"Ain't earned none yet. I got a nicked leg, but never mind that. We'll just take our horses an' git along." The man kept his rifle pointed straight at Diamond as he talked. His two friends turned to go for their horses as the lanky man backed away. Diamond was so furious he'd probably have shot him, but he didn't get the chance. The man disappeared into the darkness and a few moments later Diamond heard their horses moving away.

He was almost beside himself with rage. He went on to his horse and got the coal-oil cans. He carried them back toward the cabin, skirting the clearing so that he could come up on one blind side of the house without being seen.

Now he was down to five, and Gebhardt wasn't worth a damn. Which left himself, his two sons, and Harrison, whose head had been grazed earlier. He called, "Harrision, I want you over here."

The man came shuffling through the brush. Diamond said, "Rudy, you and Hugo see that Logan keeps his damn head down."

When Harrison reached him Diamond said, "I'll boost you up on the roof. Pour a whole gallon of coal oil over it. Those cedar shingles ought to catch like grass." He handed Harrison a coal-oil can.

Harrison said, "You're going to let them come out, aren't you?"

"Why should I? Did Logan give Reese a chance?"

Harrison put down the coal-oil can. He said, "I reckon I feel like those three new boys did. This is where you and me part company."

For a moment, Diamond was too stunned to reply. Then fury drove everything else from his mind. Harrison said, "Easy, boss. I'm just goin' to back away an' get my horse. I'll take him back to the ranch and swap him for my own. You owe me some back pay, but I reckon I can get along without any more of your money."

Diamond was trembling with rage but there was nothing he could do. He had a coal-oil can in his right hand and Harrison had a rifle pointing straight at him.

Harrison backed away. Like the other three, he disappeared into the darkness, and a few moments later Diamond heard the sound of his horse.

He yelled, "Gebhardt!"

The old choreman came toward him, crouching so as not to make himself much of a target for Logan in the house. Diamond asked belligerently, "You going to quit too?"

"No, sir."

"Then let me boost you up on the roof. I want you to pour this can of coal oil over it and then come down again."

Gebhardt picked up the can Harrison had put down and followed Diamond to the side of the house. He wished he had the courage to do what the three new men and Harrison had done, but he did not. He was too old to get another job. Nobody would hire a man as old and crippled up as he was.

Diamond boosted him up on the roof, which had a shallow pitch. This was the north side of the house, and snow had been pretty well kept blown off it during both the first storm and this one. Gebhardt poured the coal oil over the roof. It had a strong smell and made the shingles slippery. He sat down and slid off the roof, landing on his feet on the ground. The jolt hurt him but he made no sound.

Diamond left him, was gone quite a while, and returned with a huge forkful of hay. He laid it against the side of the house, poured the other can of coal oil on it, and then lighted it.

Flame raced through the hay, up the wall of the house, and across the roof. The darkness was suddenly nearly as light as day.

Diamond stood back and watched with satisfaction. Eventually the coal oil burned itself out and the flames died down. But the shingles were burning vigorously, the flames fanned by the strong wind out of the north, and there were places where it looked as if some of the logs had caught.

Diamond said, "Now let's get back there and wait for them to come out of their den."

CHAPTER TWENTY

───◆───

Mike Logan knew, long before he saw the flames, that Diamond had coal oil out there and was pouring it on the house. It had a strong, distinctive smell that even reached into the bedroom where Martha was with her two children.

He heard her call, "Mike?"

"What?"

"He's got coal oil, hasn't he?"

"Uh-huh. I think he's pouring it on the roof. I hear somebody walking around up there."

She didn't say anything after that. She didn't want to frighten her children any more than they already were. Mike knew he could hold out for a while. But he didn't dare wait so long that escape from the house would be impossible for Martha and the kids. He'd have to surrender himself before that and let Diamond do whatever he wanted to with him.

He didn't have a watch, so he had no way of knowing what time it was, and he couldn't see the stars enough to make a guess. But it seemed as if enough time has passed for Farnham to reach town, and for the sheriff and DeVoe to get back here.

The shooting had died down considerably about the time he smelled the coal oil, and once he'd thought he heard horses, but he could not be sure. Suddenly orange light fell on the brush at the far side of the clearing and on the clearing itself. Mike caught a glimpse of a man out there, and fired. He saw dirt shower into the man's face, and he knew he had undershot and had probably only filled the man's eyes with dirt.

It seemed to him that there couldn't be more than three men shooting out there, and that puzzled him. For several minutes the whole yard was nearly as bright as day. Mike raised up once to try to get a shot, but a bullet came at him instantly so close he felt the air of its passage against his neck. He ducked down immediately.

Gradually the light of the fire died down as the coal oil burned itself out. Still enough firelight remained, however, to tell Mike the roof had caught and that it was only a matter of time before it burned through. When it did, it would be only a short time before all the house's occupants would be overcome, either by the smoke or by the heat.

His time had about run out. The sheriff and his deputy weren't going to reach here in time. Now, before he was driven out, he could, perhaps, bargain with Diamond for Martha's life and for that of her two little kids. If he waited, Diamond might not be willing to bargain at all.

As swiftly as he could with his ferociously aching shoulder, he crawled away from the window and back to where Martha was. "Looks like it's over. I can't wait in here until we all die from the smoke and heat. I'm going to try and make a deal with him to let you and the kids go if I give myself up."

"No!" She came scrambling out from beneath the bed. "If you do that, I'm going with you. He won't dare kill a woman and two children and he won't dare kill you if we're watching him!"

Mike said, "You don't know him. I've hurt him too much for him to let me live. And he can't let you live to give testimony against him. Can't you see that? He'll kill us and then throw us all back into the burning house."

"Then there's no use trying to bargain with him. He won't agree, and even if he did, he wouldn't keep his word. He can't afford to let any of us live."

Mike had to admit that she was right. His mind was like that of an animal in a cage, questing, probing, looking for some way out.

Suddenly he remembered the small hatchet that Martha always kept either in or near the woodbox for splitting pieces of wood too large to go into the stove. He said, "Wait right here. Don't move and don't make a sound. I've got an idea, but I haven't got much time."

Swiftly he crawled back to the window. He snatched Farnham's rifle, then crawled rapidly across the room to the stove. He found the hatchet and went immediately to the rear wall of the house.

This was an old cabin, and this end of it was dug slightly into the hillside. Mike thought the flooring might be beginning to rot back here and he immediately discovered that he was right. It crumbled under the hatchet blows and as soon as he had made a hole big enough to insert a hand he did so and began breaking the rotten boards away.

Disregarding his orders, Martha came from the bedroom, leaving the terrified children there. Mike's shoulder hurt him so badly that every time he pulled at a board he nearly cried out with pain. But he gritted his teeth and continued, and Martha began throwing aside the debris and helping all she could.

Bullets still came in through the windows and doors, but they seemed to be striking either above their heads or over closer to the stove. After ten minutes of frantic work, Mike had a hole big enough to admit his body.

Now he chopped away just as frantically at the soft soil that had been beneath the floor. The hole he was digging grew deeper and deeper, and again Martha helped remove the dirt and debris as frantically as Mike dug it out. The hole deepened. Once, winded and panting and feeling his shoulder again soaked with blood, he paused and whispered, "How far down into the hillside is this wall?"

"I don't think more than one log is buried. There are rocks under that for a foundation, but I think just one layer of them."

Mike stopped digging down, and began to dig outward toward the wall. He struck the buried log, then, just below it, struck a rock.

Trying to pry it loose, he pulled back and could feel the heat in the room and choked suddenly on the smoke. Martha was coughing occasionally but he couldn't hear the kids. He supposed the smoke had not yet reached the bedroom, and down close to the floor was the place it would get to last.

He had to dig around the rock with the hatchet before he could get it out, but when he did, he immediately felt a blast of cold air. He was through! Now all he had to do was enlarge the hole enough to get out.

No longer did he dare use the hatchet, for fear the noise of it striking rock would be heard by those outside. Now he had to pry each foundation rock loose. But at last he had enough of them out. He said, "Go get the kids and dress them warm. But make them be quiet no matter what you have to do."

Martha departed, crawling on hands and knees, trying to stay below the thick layer of choking smoke that lay in the room and billowed out the broken windows.

Mike was already on his way out of the hole. He shoved his rifle out first, and followed it. He was exhausted, sweating heavily, dirty, and in pain. But for all that, a small smile touched his mouth, because this was so fitting. Diamond had said he'd run Mike down like a wolf. And he had. He'd run the wolf to his den, but the wolf had dug himself out. And in a few minutes the hunter was going to become the hunted.

Out in the cold, snow-laden wind, Mike crouched beside the hole he had dug, looking to right and left, ready to fire at anything that moved. In a moment, Martha came crawling out, then turned and helped the children out, one after the other. Julie started to say something, but her mother clamped a hand instantly over her mouth.

Mike pointed away from the house, toward the nearest underbrush. He put a finger to his lips. Martha acted as if she wanted to protest, but then she took each of the children by a hand and, crouching and hurrying, led them away from the burning house. She and the children were both clearly visible for several moments, but apparently Diamond and his men were watching the front of the house too closely and did not see. Martha and the children safely reached the underbrush.

Mike couldn't understand the failure of the sheriff and his deputy to come. But he did know that if he didn't get Diamond now, this would have to be done all over again. Diamond would not give up until he had killed Mike. Mike could not give up until he had killed Diamond. It had become as simple as that.

He had four bullets in his rifle now, and five in his revolver, which wasn't much good in light like this. Carefully he eased away from the cabin, trying to keep it between himself and his enemies.

He didn't know where Martha was. He couldn't see her anymore. He wished he'd told her to keep going until she was a good distance from the burning house. He suspected she'd stay, to watch, to know what finally happened to him.

Carefully, carefully he backed away. One way or another, this was going to be over soon. He was going to die, or he was going to win, and as far as the next twenty-four hours were concerned, there wouldn't be much difference. He was going to sleep like he was dead as soon as he got to a bed.

But there was no time now for weariness or pain. He had to be stronger, more silent, and more cunning in the next few minutes than he had ever been in his life before. He had to find Diamond first, he had to face him, and he had to kill the man before Diamond could kill him.

He was now out of the circle of light cast by the burning house. He moved off to his left, staying far enough so that the light wouldn't fall on him, testing each footfall before putting down his weight.

It seemed to take forever to get halfway around the house. But when he did, he heaved a long, satisfied sigh. He could hear and see the horses of Diamond and his men between him and the creek, which meant that Diamond and his men were now between him and the house.

With even more caution than before, he crept, a slow step at a time, toward the burning house. Suddenly, without warning, a section of the roof collapsed. A shower of sparks rose twenty or thirty feet into the air.

Mike heard Diamond yell triumphantly, "There! By God, they'll be comin' out of there now!"

By Diamond's voice, Mike placed him, and moved toward the sound, and an instant later saw Diamond's hulking shape crouching behind a clump of brush. Diamond held a rifle in both hands, ready to raise it the instant he saw anybody come plunging from the house. Mike realized in that instant, and finally believed, that Diamond would not have let Martha and her children go free. He couldn't afford to. They would be witnesses to arson and murder and too dangerous to be allowed to live.

Mike could have shot Diamond in the back. He could have killed him instantly. Furthermore, he knew that was what Diamond would have done to him if their positions had been reversed.

But he couldn't do it. It wasn't in him to kill a man that way. It was hard enough to kill; impossible to murder in cold blood.

He said, "Diamond. I'm here."

Diamond didn't get out of his crouch. He started violently and then he tried literally to fling himself around. Mike raised his rifle, pointing it. Diamond's rifle came level almost simultaneously.

In Diamond's eyes, just before he fired, Mike saw complete bafflement. Diamond had thought he had Mike trapped in the burning house. He had never taken his eyes off the front two windows and the door, and he'd had a man watching the bedroom window to make sure Mike didn't get out that way.

Diamond was destined never to know. Mike's bullet tore full into the center of his chest, ripping into his heart and stilling it instantly.

The force of the bullet, striking his breastbone, threw him back as if he had been kicked by a mule. He sprawled out on his back, a little wisp of smoke curling up from the muzzle of his gun. Mike couldn't even recall having heard it fire. He didn't know where the bullet had gone.

Nearest him now was Gebhardt, who threw down his rifle and stood up. He raised his hands, his face terror-filled, but also filled with the same surprise and disbelief that Diamond's had worn.

Mike shouted, "Rudy? Hugo? The old man's dead. You want to drop it now?"

He heard horses' hooves, and he heard a woman's cry. Glancing in the direction of the sounds, he saw Bondy and DeVoe riding past the burning house and behind them Martha running, dragging a child along with each hand.

Bondy said, "We got here as quick as we could."

Mike looked up and saw that both their horses were lathered. They *had* come as quickly as they could. It had just seemed that time was passing faster than it really was.

Martha reached him. She let go of her children, who each immediately hugged one of his legs. Very gently, seeing the blood and knowing how he hurt, she reached up with both hands to gently touch his unshaven face. He felt dizzy and he put his weight on her, and after a little while he was being helped into a buckboard filled with hay and she was beside him as the rig jolted back toward town.

It was over now. No longer was he a hunted animal. He looked up at the blurr of her face, raised a hand and touched it to be sure it was really there, and then he closed his eyes and slept.